Julien Roux

ICE BLUE EYES

THE SUMMER I LOST MY INNOCENCE

self-publishing

I sincerely thank the people who continuously motivated me to write and complete this novel. A special thanks goes out to Lori and Jana.

Imprint

Cover Design by: Julien Roux
 ISBN: 9798337860848 | Imprint: Independently published

Feel free to reach out if you're interested or have any questions! You can contact me at julienrouxbooks@gmail.com.

Notes

This book was originally published in German by Julien Roux in 2023.

Julien Roux is the pseudonym of an author who has been publishing e-books and paperbacks through self-publishing since 2020.

Self-publishing means that the author independently manages the entire publication process. This allows for full creative control, ensuring the content and design reflect the author's true vision.

The recommended reading age for this story is 16 and up. The novel contains homoerotic scenes. The intimate relationship between Casper and Valentin is described in explicit detail. The book also addresses themes of depression and loss in some parts.

Let's be summer again –

this time, from the very first minute, the very first light of day – from the beginning.

Let's be freshly cut grass, sunflowers, and wildflowers lining the roadside.

Let's come together like warm rain kissing scorched asphalt.

Let me be the heat on your skin, tracing down you, drop by drop.

Let me be the sultry night and the misty dawn that wraps around you.

And then, say my name like you're no longer afraid to speak it.

Touch me like I'm yours, and look at me like you miss that last summer as much as I do.

Let's be summer together again.

Chapter 1

Arriving at the end of the world—that's what it felt like when I first stepped into that small seaside town.

The wind whipped rain against my face, cold crept under my clothes, and pure despair settled in my chest. A bleak welcome to the middle of nowhere, deep in the north, on a tiny campsite—the last place I wanted to be that summer.

Never in my wildest dreams did I imagine finding something so rare, something so unforgettable in this place. Val, that wild, one-of-a-kind boy who still lingers in my thoughts over a year later.

Val was like the weather by the North Sea—untamed and cold like the crashing waves, yet in a moment, he could be warm and inviting, utterly irresistible like the first rays of spring sunshine.

*

I still can't understand what my parents were thinking—taking us on a trip to the North Sea in a cramped camper van. Two whole weeks of being packed like sardines, with the typical miserable weather as the cherry on top.

They might as well have suggested going straight to Antarctica; neither place holds anything remotely interesting for me.

My original plan was to head to San Sebastián with my friends Josh and Elli for kite camp, just like last year. Back to where Luuk, the ridiculously hot Dutch kite instructor, would be again this year.

Last summer, there was definitely something between Luuk and me – the way he looked at me when he thought I wasn't watching, the way he'd casually put his hand on my shoulder when no one was around. I didn't imagine any of it. More could've happened last summer if I'd only had the guts to take it further. But back then, everything was different; I was still clueless and inexperienced.

I was certain that this year, something would've finally happened between us—if I'd just been given the chance. But after the mess I got myself into thanks to Charlie, my parents pulled the plug on the kite camp and dragged me, against my will, to the chilly northern coast of Germany.

It was already storming on the drive there. I couldn't even begin to imagine surviving a single day in such a dreary place, let alone in a camper van.

The camper technically belongs to my aunt, but this year, she offered it to us for our summer vacation. My dad jumped at the idea, thrilled at the notion of a 'family camping trip.' He was convinced it would 'bring the family closer together'—especially us kids.

My sisters, Lina and Larissa—the fraternal twins who are two years younger than me—have made my life hell for as long as I can remember. They're attention-seeking, always breaking my stuff, and throw fits whenever they're not the center of attention.

We have nothing in common. They're into pop music; I'm all about punk. They're horse-crazy; I'm into skating and surfing. This vacation was already shaping up to be a complete nightmare for me.

*

We arrived in the pouring rain, and of course, I had to help my dad set up the camper. Within minutes, my clothes were soaked, sticking to my skin while I cursed under my breath – which, naturally, my dad completely ignored. Nothing ever fazes him, unlike my mom. We're always at odds. But at least once we finished and changed, he gave me a knowing wink and slipped me a couple of fifty-euro bills.

'I heard there's a kite school nearby. You could probably use this there.'

'Sure,' I muttered, managing a quick 'thanks.' It's better than nothing. I'm always broke, and my parents hardly ever give us anything extra. We don't get allowances. Ever since I turned 13, I've had to earn everything myself. I started with a paper route and more recently picked up shifts as a waiter at a small café near our place. But thanks to their holiday plans, I can kiss that job goodbye for now. My parents have money – more than enough that I wouldn't need to take on every side gig – but they're all about teaching us to earn everything ourselves. 'Life doesn't give out freebies,' as they like to say.

It's tough being 16 and watching your friends easily buy the latest Nikes, upgrade to the newest phones, or pay for gym memberships while you're stuck feeling like an idiot because you can't afford any of it.

*

The campsite sits right by the beach, with only the dike separating us from the shore. Looking out at the site through the pouring rain doesn't exactly lift my spirits. Everything's blurred and gray, like the whole place is slowly sinking under the deluge.

A little farther off, I notice a restaurant with a thatched roof and the typical red-brick exterior. Above the door, a brown rooster sign swings wildly in the wind, with the name beneath it: The Wild Rooster. The name sounds as odd as the entire town looks.

Warm light spills from the narrow windows, the only hint of coziness in this bleak setting.

"I think I'll grab something to eat," I mutter as my stomach growls in agreement.

"Good idea," my dad says, following me inside.

The place is packed – it seems like every tourist and local in town has taken refuge here from the weather.

Snatches of conversation, loud laughter, the clatter of cutlery and glasses fill the air.

The Wild Rooster is rustic, all wood, aiming for a ship's cabin vibe. Anchors, stuffed fish, and boat ropes decorate the walls. I sigh, hoping they at least serve something normal like schnitzel and fries.

My dad lucks out and finds two seats on the left side, where the staff rushes back and forth between the dining area and the kitchen.

With the cash in my pocket, I could easily sneak something strong without Dad noticing. The thought gives me a boost.

"I'm getting us drinks," I say, weaving through the crowd toward the bar.

The instant I spot the flash of blue hair, my pulse quickens.

A guy, unfortunately with his back to me, stands there. He's lean, dressed in a blue t-shirt that perfectly matches his striking hair, with a silver chain glinting around his neck. I'm not sure why, but that little detail grabs my attention. The shaved nape of his neck, the way his shoulders are slightly raised, his straight, confident posture – it all holds me in place for a moment.

I clear my throat, half hoping he'll be the one to serve me.

Then he turns, and I'm met with a face that catches me off guard – mostly because of the open irritation in his eyes. They lock onto mine, cold and unfriendly, sizing me up in one quick glance. He's clearly not interested in playing nice, and I can feel the judgment in his look, like he's trying to figure out if I'm just another clueless tourist.

I try to convey with my eyes that I'm not here to waste his time, that I understand – working a shift like this, dealing with tourists, must be rough. But my silent message doesn't seem to land. His left eyebrow, pierced with a tiny hoop, arches as if to say, You're still in my way. He leans in slightly, hovering over the bar just enough to hear me better.

For some reason, I freeze, unable to find my voice. I just stare at him, taking in every detail, completely mesmerized.

Damn it, he's beautiful – not in the conventional way, but there's something about him that sets him apart from the crowd of tourists and locals.

His skin is pale like porcelain, with a beauty mark above his lips. His forehead, chin, and cheeks are sprinkled with faint birthmarks, like a map leading to his eyes – eyes that are a piercing blue, bright and intense, pulling me in like they're reading straight into my soul.

Then there's his mouth, lips that look like they'd taste of cherries, summer heat, and sweet rebellion. I'm already lost in a daydream when his sharp voice slices through my thoughts.

"What?" he snaps, bursting the fantasy bubble I didn't even realize I was floating in.

"I, uh, I'll have a vodka," I say, flashing a cheeky grin, determined not to let this opportunity slip away.

He snorts, leaning against the bar, and I notice how the muscles in his forearms flex, revealing a few scattered tattoos against his pale skin. I find myself wondering, *What's a guy like him doing in a place like this?*

"You're joking, right?" His tone is thick with skepticism.

"Why not?" I shoot back, adding a playful wink.

That eyebrow arches again, and now I catch a glimpse of lighter strands beneath the blue—probably his natural blond.

"You're not even close to legal drinking age," he says with a weary sigh, wiping a bit of sweat from his forehead. It's clear he's been working hard – probably a double shift. The apron tied over his t-shirt is already stained from the chaos of serving drinks, but none of it dulls his pride or that undeniable allure.

I swallow hard, forcing myself not to stare too blatantly. "I'll be seventeen soon," I challenge, the thought of lying briefly flickering in my mind. But something about him makes me want to be straight-up. Instead, I give him a wide-eyed, hopeful look – the kind that usually works like magic back in the city. But with him, it doesn't even make a dent.

"Then you're not getting anything," he replies flatly, grabbing a glass and a towel, ready to move on.

Acting on a sudden, crazy impulse, I reach out and grab his wrist. His skin is warm, smooth, and it sends a shiver straight through me. I gasp, unable to let go as my heart starts pounding in my chest.

He jerks back slightly, eyes flashing with something – anger? Shock? I can't tell. My mind goes blank, but all I can feel is the wild rhythm of my heartbeat.

"Forget it," he mutters, but even the irritation in his voice can't pull me out of the haze I'm floating in.

"No worries, it's cool," I mumble, flashing him a grin that's half-nervous, half-hopeful. "So, when's your shift over?"

Bold, I know, but I can't resist. This might be my one chance to get to know him.

He hesitates, clearly confused, glancing from my hand on his wrist back to my eyes. Slowly, I release my grip, but I'm not ready to back down just yet.

"Come on, it's probably boring as hell around here at night, right? Is there anything cool to do in this town?" I ask, tossing in another wink.

He shrugs, setting the glass down and turning to rinse some dirty cups in the sink. For a moment, I just watch him work – the way he moves with a calm precision, like nothing else exists around him. Every now and then, he glances at me, but I can't move. I'm stuck, waiting for him to make the next move, unwilling to walk away until I get what I came for – him.

Suddenly, an older woman elbows her way in beside me, bumping my shoulder hard. I shoot her an annoyed glare, but she just presses in closer, trying to grab the blue-haired bartender's attention. Determined to beat her to it, I lean over the counter, propping myself up with my elbows.

"Do you ever get a break?" I purr.

He sighs, leaning back, and our eyes lock as he studies me, clearly weighing his answer while I get lost in the icy blue depths of his gaze.

We're so damn close now. I can smell him – a mix of hard work and something fresh, like saltwater and sun-warmed skin. That wild, free scent wraps around me, making me grin like an idiot.

"Why are you so interested?" he asks, amusement lacing his words.

I smirk back, making sure he catches the meaning. If he wasn't interested, he wouldn't still be leaning so close.

"So, are you in?" I ask, making it as obvious as I can.

The noise around us is almost deafening, and the woman beside me waves her bright-red nails in front of my face, still trying to cut in.

"We'd like a large bottle of water," she yells over the noise. I glare at her, but she just glares right back.

The blue-haired guy slams a bottle onto the counter, shoves it her way, and takes her money without so much as blinking. She huffs and storms off, bottle in hand.

I look back at him, and a smirk curls at the corner of his mouth.

"I don't have a free evening until two days from now. We could meet at the pier around seven," he says.

"Sounds good," I reply, ready to say more, but he turns away, cutting me off.

I'm left wondering what that was all about – is this a date or just a distraction for both of us? Does he even realize I'm flirting? And more importantly, is he into guys? I don't know his name, his age, or anything about him, but my mind is already racing with possibilities.

Is he local? What's he doing working here? He doesn't seem like he belongs in a place like this. If I had to live and work here, I'd feel just as trapped.

I head back to our table, having completely forgotten to order drinks. Luckily, my dad isn't as distracted as I am and already ordered Cokes and food.

Even as we eat, I can't tear my eyes away from him.

He stands out in every way – not just because of his blue hair. He's like a vibrant splash of color in an otherwise dull scene, and everything about him is just a little too perfect. The rough, grumpy attitude he shows the other guests only adds to his appeal. Smiling is definitely not in his playbook.

At one point, I see a thickset man pull him aside, gesturing wildly as he talks. I watch as the blue-haired boy just shrugs it off, unfazed. That must be his boss, but it clearly doesn't bother him. He doesn't change the way he interacts with anyone, not even a bit.

The food – schnitzel and fries in my case – turns out better than expected, and my dad even lets me have a beer. I would've loved to talk to him again, but I don't get the chance. Not tonight.

*

After dinner with my father, I headed through the rain to the kite school on the beach and signed up for the course. At least it gets me out of the cramped RV for a while. The whole sleeping situation is just too intense.

My sisters sleep in a bunk bed, and I sleep across from them in a single bed that I have to fold up every day to make room for sitting and eating. Up front is the double bed where my parents sleep, which also has to be dismantled every day to save space.

It's super annoying, but that's not even the worst part. The real issue is that we all have to sleep in the same room. My dad snores, my sisters refuse to go to bed, staying up half the night reading or glued to their phones, and then sleep until noon. I toss and turn all night, and I'm getting to the point where I seriously consider sleeping outside on the beach just to get some rest. Only the wind and rain stop me.

After just one night, I'm completely exhausted and end up napping in a beach chair by the sea. Since kitesurfing depends on the tide, the courses only start in the afternoon.

*

The kite course is turning out to be way better than I expected. I'm stepping onto the beach with the cool ocean breeze hitting my face, and right away, I'm feeling a relaxed, friendly vibe from the group. Everyone is about my age, laughing, chatting, and already getting along like we've known each other for more than just a few hours. The instructors are only a couple of years older than us, and they're just as laid-back, making the whole experience feel less like a class and more like hanging out with a bunch of friends.

It's the first place that's giving me a glimmer of hope that maybe this vacation won't be as dull as I feared. Maybe, just maybe, there's something here that can make my time worthwhile.

I'm joining the advanced group right off the bat, thanks to my experience from the kite camp last year, and Maddie, a blonde girl my age with an infectious energy, is in the same group. We click instantly, sharing inside jokes and pushing each other to do better, which makes everything a lot more fun.

I'm spending most of my time out on the water, letting the wind catch my kite and pull me across the waves, the adrenaline surging through me with every jump and turn. It feels amazing—this freedom, this rush of flying over the water—but even in those moments of pure joy, I can't shake the thought of him. The boy with the bright blue hair. Every time I'm floating above the waves, the sound of seagulls screeching overhead and the saltwater spraying my skin, my mind keeps wandering back to him.

Why can't I get him out of my head? His image keeps popping into my thoughts at the most random times. I'm riding the waves, the wind is at my back, and suddenly, there he is, flashing in my mind. I'm wondering who he really is, what his story is. There's something about him, something I can't quite put my finger on, that keeps pulling me in. I wish I knew more, could somehow get closer to him, find out what's beneath that distant exterior.

As the day goes on, between kiteboarding sessions and hanging out with the group, I'm constantly thinking about the next evening. I'm really looking forward to it, almost like I'm counting down the hours. I'm trying not to get my hopes up, though. Part of me is convinced he won't even show, but the other part, the part that's still hoping, is holding on to the idea that maybe he will.

That's what's keeping me going through the day—the idea of maybe, just maybe, seeing him again. There's this restless energy bubbling under the surface, a quiet anticipation that's hard to ignore. It's strange, really, how someone I barely know is taking up so much space in my thoughts.

My second night in the camper, and my mind's all over the place, making up these scenarios I know probably won't happen, but I can't stop imagining them. We're on the beach, sitting next to each other in one of those beat-up beach chairs, the sun going down behind us. I picture myself reaching over, sliding my hand under his shirt, feeling the smooth skin on his stomach. I can see his muscles twitch when I touch him, like he's caught off guard but doesn't pull away.

In my head, I lean in closer, feeling his warmth, and press my lips to his neck, then his mouth. I can almost taste him—something sweet, with that salty ocean air. I imagine him melting into me, the hesitation slipping away, his lips soft at first and then more intense, like he's been holding back, just like me.

He's so hot, but at the same time, it's like he's untouchable—distant, hard to figure out. Even when he's right there, he feels miles away. And I can't stop thinking about how to close that distance, how to make this daydream real.

But deep down, I know it's probably not gonna happen. After another sleepless night tossing around in the cramped camper, I'm just frustrated. I can't stop thinking about him, hoping that maybe—just maybe—he's been thinking about me too. That somehow, he wants what I want.

On the outside, we don't seem to match at all—he's this tall, blue-haired mystery with perfect skin, and I'm just this black-haired 16-year-old kid with way too much imagination. It's like we're from two different worlds, standing right next to each other.

Does he even see me that way? Does he think the way I do? I'm lying here, practically aching for him, and I don't even know if I'm on his radar like that. It's killing me, not knowing. Does he want me the way I want him, or am I just setting myself up for something that's never gonna happen?

Chapter 2

My parents are giving me more freedom here. I can pretty much do whatever I want, which is so different from back home where they're always watching me. I can't even go to the skate park anymore without my mom kicking off a lecture.

It wasn't always like this between us. We used to get along, and my mom probably would've trusted me with anything. But that changed when I met Charlie at the skate park. Everything felt so easy with him—skating, dealing with life, and handling whatever crap got thrown our way. He lived with his older sister in a tiny apartment in a much poorer residential area and, just like me, was always broke.

Still, he always wore brand-new Nike shoes and designer clothes. It didn't take me long to figure out how.

Charlie had a real knack for making things "disappear" without ever getting caught. With Charlie, everything seemed so easy – whether it was skating or stealing. And like an idiot, I thought I could handle that "talent" just as well as he could.

For a while, it worked. I'd walk out of stores with new clothes or shoes, trying to look casual, even when the alarm went off. But then I got caught red-handed trying to swipe a pair of fresh Nike Airs.

That didn't stop me from hanging out with Charlie though.

We turned night into day, cruising through the city on our boards. Nothing was off-limits. We tagged walls and trains, snuck into clubs and concerts through back entrances and rooftops, and never paid a cent—booze, smokes, and everything else came 'free' thanks to Charlie.

It was like an addiction, the ultimate adrenaline rush – how much further could we go? What else could we get away with?

Charlie knew no limits, and he dragged me right along with him, straight to the edge. We were both drunk the night everything went to hell, but I was way more wasted than he was. Charlie thought it'd be fun to hurl rocks from a construction site through the windows of a flower shop in the town square and then steal the cash register.

He threw, I didn't. I just stood there like an idiot and let him do it, didn't stop him. I started feeling sick. The nausea got worse when the shop's alarm went off and the police sirens got closer. I tried to run, but Charlie was way faster – much faster.

He got away. I got caught. After that, he vanished just as quickly as he'd appeared at the skate park that first time. I, on the other hand, crashed hard into reality.

One freezing night in a cell because I didn't have an ID on me, followed by a charge for vandalism. Only thanks to my parents and a large sum of money was the flower shop owner's complaint eventually dropped.

That was nearly a year ago, and yeah, I regret it – every single thing. Acting like a total idiot, not caring about anything, and being a complete jerk.

There's still a huge rift of mistrust between my parents and me—one that's hard to fix. I should be glad they're giving me more freedom here, at least for now. But they also know there's not much trouble I can get into in this tiny place.

I had to leave my skateboard at home, I don't have a bike, and there's nowhere I can really go on foot without getting blisters.

Kiteboarding and lying on the beach are the only things I can do outside the campsite – and looking out for him.

I got lucky once.

The morning after our encounter, I saw him in front of the restaurant around midday.

He was holding two full trash bags. It seemed like he was just about to take a break because as soon as he tossed the bags into the large black bins, he grabbed a red bike leaning against the restaurant's brick wall and rode off.

That same untouchable aura surrounded him again, and he looked effortlessly cool with sunglasses on, a beanie pulled over his head, and a brightly colored t-shirt – this time in pink. The same pudgy man from the restaurant suddenly burst out of the back door and yelled after him in anger, but he didn't even look back, just kept riding over the dike.

His attitude – that "screw all of you" vibe – fascinated me, even though I have a feeling it's only going to lead to pain and heartache for me in the end.

*

Luckily, my parents didn't ask any questions when I threw on my jacket at 7 PM, mumbled a quick goodbye, and headed to the pier.

The pier is the town's main hub, along with the Wild Rooster. The wooden structure stretches out into the sea, lined with small souvenir shops and food stalls. But by now, everything's closed—it feels like the sidewalks roll up at 6 PM around here.

I force myself to walk slowly, not wanting to look too eager in case he's watching. I keep my eyes down most of the time, hands buried deep in my jacket pockets, afraid to let myself hope.

I'm pretty sure he didn't mean the shops here when he mentioned the meeting spot, but the end of the pier, where there's a wide view over the sea and the beach below.

I don't even glance up on the way there, I'm so damn nervous. One look could shatter all the hope I've built up over the past two days. So, it's only when I'm almost at my destination that I finally dare to look up.

But all I see is an old couple standing there, gazing out at the sea.

Great, I scold myself inwardly. He didn't show. I knew it.

Annoyed, I step next to them, lean against the railing, and look down. I let my gaze drift over the sea and the wide beach. Then suddenly, I freeze. Barely visible among the dunes, I spot a distinct blue smudge that looks out of place from up here.

My pulse immediately starts racing. I spin around and rush forward way too fast until I feel the sand beneath my shoes.

From down here, the blue smudge is gone, but I know I'm heading in the right direction.

I find the beautiful stranger among the sand dunes in the restricted area marked off for conservation.

Once again, he's wearing a light-colored t-shirt, this time in pink, which makes him look even paler, almost ghostly, like he's not really there. He's holding a cigarette butt in his hand, and I can smell its contents before I even reach him. I can't help but grin.

But when he spots me, he visibly flinches and mutters something under his breath.

Did he forget? Yeah, probably.

But now that I've finally found him, relief takes over, and I ignore his gruff attitude, dropping onto his large towel without being invited and mumbling a "Hi."

He looks at me, puzzled.

"Were we supposed to meet?"

I snort.

"Yep."

"Ah..." He looks around as if expecting someone else to be behind me.

"Alright then."

He doesn't sound the least bit excited, and with those words, he leans forward, turning slightly away from me as he takes another drag on his joint before twisting it shut and hiding it in his palm.

I roll my eyes internally but say nothing, just like he doesn't. An awkward silence settles between us. The stranger seems practiced at this – it doesn't seem to bother him at all.

His eyes stay calmly fixed on the sea and the crashing waves while I stare at him, full of questions. I try to resist the urge to get up and leave, along with the frustration building inside me from his arrogant and rough demeanor. Somehow, I'm convinced there's more behind this façade. At least, I hope there is.

"What's your name anyway?" I finally ask.

He tilts his head slightly but only meets my gaze briefly.

"Val," he murmurs before taking another drag on the remnants of his joint. Then he snuffs it out with a sigh.

"And you?" He forces the question out like he couldn't care less.

"Cas," I reply.

He raises his left eyebrow.

"And the full name?"

"Casper, but that's too long..." I don't like the full version for obvious reasons. Who wants to be named after a ghost or a puppet show character?

He pulls a face like someone just bit him.

"Shit, you're serious?"

I don't reply. I've been teased about my name enough times that I don't even mention the full version anymore. Not even my ex, Finn, ever asked about it. Maybe that's part of why we never really got deep.

"Who'd want to be named that," he mutters, and I already regret being so honest with him.

"With a C, not a K." By now, this conversation is getting on my nerves. I don't need to justify myself to a near-stranger.

"Doesn't make any difference to me." He looks away, completely disinterested. I really should just get up and leave. This is a total waste of time, but something inside me still holds a tiny spark of hope.

No one's an asshole for no reason, and Val's too young to be a complete one.

I sit up a bit and look at him.

"And you? Val?"

"What about it?"

"Guaranteed it's a nickname too," I guess.

He snorts, takes a deep breath, and shrugs.

"Valentin," he mutters, much quieter now. At least he didn't beat around the bush, though it's not what I expected. Patron saint of lovers – his mom couldn't have picked a less fitting name for the ice block next to me. I can't help but grin inside.

"Perfect name for you," I say with a wink.

A sudden chill runs through me – a realization.

We have something in common: our names aren't exactly judgment-free, and I'm sure he's had to endure his share of comments because of it too. And yet he just told me without hesitation.

First, I smirk, then I burst out laughing, unable to hold back the laughter bubbling up from my throat.

Val looks at me, skeptical, his lips pursed in annoyance. It only makes me want to laugh even more.

Giggling, I cover my mouth to keep from laughing out loud.

"Seriously?" he snorts, shaking his head in disbelief.

"Yep. If you think Casper's bad, then I'll just call you Valentin from now on."

"Alright then, Casper," he grumbles.

"Okay, I can live with that," I grin.

He shakes his head again, staring at me like I'm crazy. But he doesn't get up and leave, so I take that as a win.

"You're pretty weird, but you probably already know that."

I just shrug.

"So, where are you from anyway?" he asks next.

I wiggle my eyebrows. "What do you think?"

"No idea, but definitely not from here."

"Maybe I'm just a figment of your imagination, conjured up by that joint of yours."

He rolls his eyes.

"A man from the sea," I add with a giggle.

"Yeah, right, you joker. I clearly remember you trying to sabotage my only free evening two days ago."

"Sabotage, is that what you call it?" I tease him.

"What else would you call whatever you're pulling right now?"

I shrug.

"I'll tell you when I figure it out."

"Uh-huh." He tilts his head doubtfully and reaches out to dig his hand into the sand next to the towel.

"And you? Do you really live here?"

He rolls his eyes.

"Why do you want to know so badly?"

"Well, I mean, all I know is your name – your full name." I smirk again, and Val responds with an eye roll.

"You're way too nosy."

I wink at him, but this time he completely ignores it. He actually seems more agitated now.

"So?" he snaps. "What else do you want to know? How tall I am, how old, how much I weigh? When I last got laid?"

I gasp in surprise.

"Damn," I blurt out. "Are you always this moody?"

He leans back, falling onto his elbows, tilts his head back, and just stares up at the sky, completely ignoring me.

"Yeah, pretty much," he finally says, way too late.

"Why?"

He leans back further, resting his head on the towel. Taking a deep breath, he closes his eyes, and I can't help but stare. His golden eyelashes, the flutter of his lids, the slight trembling of his red lips. Just beautiful.

"It's easier that way," he says quietly, opening his eyes and locking them onto mine. I flinch, like I've been jolted. I swallow hard.

No, I can't leave, can't get up. I'm too curious about him. So, I follow his lead, leaning back until I'm lying on the towel too, staring straight at him.

That pale skin, smooth as porcelain, the sharp chin and cheekbones, everything hard as razors, framed by those blazing blue eyes that now narrow with suspicion as they gaze at me.

Besides the piercings in his left ear and eyebrow, he has one in his right nostril. I'm guessing there are more, but they're probably hidden.

"No idea," I finally say when he doesn't respond, "I wait tables too. It's a tough job."

He lets out a faint grunt.

"At least you probably get a real paycheck for it."

"Sure, don't you?"

He gives me a serious look, sits up, and wraps his arms around his knees.

"Nope, it's my old man's place."

"Old man" doesn't exactly scream harmony.

"And his wife runs the kitchen, so that's already two fewer people he has to pay."

"So, you really are from here…" I summarize in a hushed, somewhat surprised voice.

"Yep, tried to get out, but couldn't, as you can see."

I nod. He sighs, looking back out toward the horizon.

"Spent almost four years in Berlin, trained as a sound engineer, worked in a big studio afterward, but then…" He trails off, and pain flickers in his light eyes.

For a moment, I search his face for an answer, waiting for him to continue.

But this time, I wait in vain. I can tell he's clearly more unsettled now. Above his hand, half-buried in the dry sand, I spot a tattoo of a flower with the letter Z next to it.

"Berlin, wow. No idea why you came back here."

He just breathes deeply, not responding again.

"And where are you from?" He looks straight at me this time.

"Straight from the campsite. My current room is barely one meter by two meters."

He rolls his eyes but doesn't laugh.

"Near the city of Bonn," I finally answer truthfully.

"Well, it's not Berlin, but it's got to be a thousand times better than this dump. No sane person would voluntarily spend even one winter here," he mutters.

"I bet. I can barely survive the summer here!"

This time, he laughs. Quiet and rough, and that rough laugh of his echoes through my body, reverberating inside me. I can see it now, that sparkle deep inside him, briefly shining through in that moment.

But then he stops.

"Why did you really want to meet me?" he asks again, eyes narrowing suspiciously.

As he says this, he turns away from me, starts rummaging in his backpack, and pulls out a small metal tin and two cans of Jever. He hands me one.

"No vodka, but I guess you're old enough to drink this."

"Not funny," I say, taking the beer from him. Our fingers brush briefly, and once again, that shiver runs through me, just like the first time I touched him at the bar. Intense, electrifying, absolutely spine-tingling.

I discreetly study him. He doesn't react at all. Is he really that cold, or is it all just an act?

"So?" he presses.

I stare at him, getting lost in that icy expression he's giving me.

Then I remember his question.

Yeah, why am I here? Why don't I just leave?

Shit, because I find him utterly fascinating and can't understand how someone so beautiful and vibrant ended up stuck in such a dreary place.

I want to know more about him, everything I can coax out of him. And there's no way I'm walking away now. Not just because he fascinates me, but because he's driving me crazy in every possible way. Especially my dick, which is pressing uncomfortably against my jeans and just won't settle down.

I'm buzzing and burning inside – just from sitting next to him. And no, I've never felt anything this intense before. Not with anyone. Not even with Finn. My ex-boyfriend. We were only together for a few weeks, but we made good use of the time, trying just about everything our imaginations could come up with.

But Finn and Val – there's no comparison. Val feels like something from another world. One that draws me in hard.

"I just wanted to get to know you," I answer evasively.

He snorts again, taking a sip of his beer.

"Why?"

He doesn't let up. Does he really have no clue? Does he not realize how he comes across to others?

"You stand out, you know that, right?"

"Because of my hair or what?" He blinks.

"No, it's like you have this aura..."

He laughs again, this time louder but still rough and jagged enough to turn me inside out.

"Aura, huh? And what kind would that be? And don't give me the whole 'blue' crap."

I grin, joining in his laughter.

" I don't know yet, that's kinda why I wanted to hang out and get to know you."

"Yeah, right." He runs his fingers over the back of his neck, rubbing the closely shaved hair at the nape. I can clearly see lighter roots growing in.

"So, what is it? What's this?" He takes another swig of beer, and I follow suit, stalling for time.

His gaze pierces into mine, and I feel like I'm walking on hot coals. He expects an answer, and I can't dodge it any longer. So, I swallow my nerves and smile at him.

"Oh, come on! I can't be the first one to ask you out," I blurt, then freeze. Crap. Why did I just say that?

Chapter 3

Val eyes me skeptically.

"You're into guys?" His voice is completely calm, but I can see the gears turning in his face, in his eyes.

I shrug, suddenly feeling exposed and helpless under his piercing gaze, as if I were standing there naked.

"Seems like it," I murmur, almost to myself. He sighs, stretches, and I catch a glimpse beneath his hoodie. Pale, smooth skin and the hint of abs. I can't help but imagine running my fingers over them right now.

"I mean–" He clears his throat. "Sure, sometimes people ask me out." He looks at me thoughtfully. "But it's always been women."

I take a sip of my beer, staring out at the horizon. By now, I'm 99% sure I've been deluding myself. Val isn't into guys, not even a little. It was all just wishful thinking on my part.

Val doesn't say anything more either, and the silence between us stretches out like a burning, uncomfortable fire that makes my heart beat even more nervously in my chest.

I need to get out of here before I make a total fool of myself – though, let's face it, I already have.

Val takes another sip of his beer, sighs, and then sits up straight, stiffly.

"I never really got it, you know, the dates and the sex…" He looks at me again. "Shit, I'm pretty messed up." He glances away, like he's talking more to himself than to me, and then lets out a dry laugh. There's a sudden sadness and loneliness in his voice.

Together, we stare at the horizon and the seagulls screeching over the sea.

I don't know what to say to that, but Val doesn't seem to expect an answer from me. Yet suddenly, I feel him turn his head, looking at me again.

I don't dare look back at him, don't dare get my hopes up. It's pointless.

"I mean, you're good-looking, so you probably don't have any trouble finding someone…"

He sounds uncertain. I know this sudden attempt at kindness is meant to comfort me, but it also feels like a clear rejection.

"It's okay, you don't need to explain," I say with a sigh.

"No, I should."

Now I look at him, confused.

"I mean… I don't know, I've never been with a guy." His teeth graze his lower lip briefly.

"It's not a requirement."

Val shrugs, then narrows his eyes.

"There's really nothing to do around here," he says quietly.

He stares at me with an intensity that makes my pulse quicken. Before I can process what's happening, his lips are suddenly on mine. Hesitant, uncertain, but curious—and, damn, so good.

Holy shit, I think to myself, how can lips feel this perfect?

Everything inside me seems to explode, every molecule spinning, swirling around.

All my feelings are laser-focused on this connection between us, the rest fading into a thick fog.

I know this is my chance – maybe the only one I'll ever get with him.

Quickly, I wrap my hand around his neck, pulling him closer, feeling the cold silver chain against his neck and beneath my trembling fingers. He pulls back slightly, as if trying to escape my touch, but when I run my tongue along his lips, he parts them, letting me slide effortlessly into his mouth.

His beautiful, red mouth on mine – such warmth radiates from it, a true fire. And his tongue – wild as it pushes against mine. I can feel the cool metal of a piercing. We embrace each other passionately; it's more of a battle than a kiss. Intense, circling, challenging, and conquering.

But Val doesn't pull away or break the kiss. So, I get bolder.

I press my fingers into his neck. My free hand twitches, wanting to feel more and more of him. I dare to slide it under his t-shirt, over his back, gently scratching his skin with my nails.

He feels so warm, so full of life. Like a magnet that's drawn me in from the moment we met. And this kiss is beyond compare, seeping into every corner of my being, enveloping me, filling me completely.

His taste in my mouth – it's a mix of hops, cinnamon gum, and something indescribable that flows through me. In that moment, I wish it would never end, that this kiss could last forever.

But just as quickly as he pressed his lips to mine, he pulls back and moves away from me.

His mouth is open, his breath brushing against my lips. He stares at me in surprise, his eyes wide and open in that moment, and I feel like I can see straight into his soul. And what I see there makes my heart race even faster.

But then he snorts, and that arrogant, distant look settles back over his mouth. His eyes narrow into tight slits.

"Okay, that was... an experience."

I swallow, his words rudely dragging me back to reality.

I look at him questioningly, pulling my trembling fingers out from under his t-shirt and staring at him.

His face is almost inhumanly beautiful, but his eyes suddenly radiate a coldness, like the sky above the clouds where the atmosphere is too thin to breathe and everything freezes, including my heart.

Val turns away, rummages through his backpack, and pulls out a metal tin. Inside are tobacco and a small bag of weed.

"Can I have some? " I ask, crossing my arms, trying to mask how much his sudden mood swings are getting under my skin.

He glances over his shoulder. "You're too young. I don't break that rule. "

I snort, frustration bubbling up. "But kissing's fine? " I snap.

He exhales heavily. "Just wanted to see if it's any different from kissing girls. "

Asshole. But I still can't resist asking, "And?"

"Yeah... it is, " he mutters, focused on rolling his joint.

I wait, but he doesn't elaborate.

"Alright," I mutter, feeling like the biggest idiot.

A sharp pang of longing pierces through me. I wish I were back in France, back in San Sebastián with my best friends. With people like Finn, who never treated my sexuality like some curiosity or experiment.

Val, despite living in Berlin, feels trapped in his own narrow worldview—or maybe he just doesn't care about me, or anything, at all.

What did he say earlier? Even the girls he was with didn't do it for him?

What's wrong with him? Does he really feel nothing? For anyone?

How can we be sitting here next to each other and feel so completely different? How is that possible? How could he not feel this trembling, this unspeakable attraction during our kiss?

I hug my knees to my chest and watch him as he continues rolling his joint. I feel so out of place next to him, here on the beach. But I can't and don't want to go back to the camper with my family either.

When he's finished, he briefly inspects his work before lighting it. With a calmness that irritates me, he smokes while gazing out at the sea, while I discreetly take a few breaths of the smoke.

"So?" he finally asks, his voice calm as he looks at me, "What's it like?"

"What?" I snort, trying to glare at him, to make him see how much I despise his arrogant attitude. But he doesn't flinch, nor does he stop asking dumb questions.

"You know, with a guy."

I groan quietly.

"If you want to know how the sex works, watch a porn and stop bothering me with it!"

I press my lips together, and even this cold blue block of ice next to me seems to finally realize how shitty it is to talk to me like that.

He raises his left eyebrow.

"Okay..." he murmurs, turning away from me and taking another drag from his joint. Then suddenly, he hands it to me.

Wordlessly, I take the little stub and finish smoking it. I do it with the same calmness, without looking at him again.

His weed is decent, tastes homegrown, not particularly strong. But it helps calm me down and keeps my mind from constantly spinning with wild theories about the guy next to me.

"Sorry, " he mutters, wrapping his arms around his knees, staring at me with a mix of regret and frustration.

I tilt my head, letting out a small snort, unsure how to respond. He blinks, almost apologetic.

"I hate it here. Everything—the place, the people. While you and the tourists get to do whatever you want, I'm stuck behind the bar at the Wild Rooster, serving drunks." He shakes his head, a quiet sigh escaping his lips.

"I thought by 21 I'd be somewhere else, seeing the world, producing killer bands. Fuck, doing something that takes me further, but then... I ended up back here, shit!" he curses.

I nod but don't say anything. I can tell there's a lot more beneath the surface. Val didn't come back here voluntarily. Definitely not. But I don't think he wants to hear any advice from me right now.

"I'm only doing this for one more season, then I'm out. I'll get the cash Frank owes me and go as far away as I can. Shit, I'd rather live on the street than rot away here any longer," he grumbles.

There's so much anger in him, so much despair. And he's sharing it with me.

Val runs a hand through his hair, letting his head fall forward. Everything here is hard for him. And yet, he's trusting me in some inexplicable way. Maybe he does feel something, at least a tiny bit, for me.

I feel a deep urge to get close to him again, really close.

Tentatively, I reach for his hand, brushing my fingers over his. He looks up, surprised, but he doesn't pull away.

"I'm not gay," he says softly, his voice rough and brittle.

"You don't have to be. I don't label myself either," I reply calmly.

"Label?"

His fingers move toward mine, intertwining with them and staying there between us. It feels so unbelievably good.

"I don't define myself by my sexuality." I look at him and can't help biting my lower lip.

I've never had a conversation like this before. I've never had to come out. Either because I've been in places where I found people like Finn, or because my friends figured out what I liked from how I acted.

"Yeah, but you're only into guys, right?" It comes out more hesitantly and cautiously now, not as careless and hurtful as before.

I shrug.

"Mostly, but is that all there is to me?"

He shakes his head and his hand gently squeezes mine.

I smile at him. "Or do you go around telling everyone you're into girls?"

Now he grins.

"Nah, shit!" A laugh escapes him, wonderfully rough and raw, honest and open.

We both look out at the sea, at the crashing waves, as the sun slowly sinks into the water, casting everything around us in an unreal fiery red-orange glow. Even Val. His pale skin seems to glow, his eyes burn.

As the last sliver disappears beyond the horizon, I feel his gaze on me again. But now it's different: curious and open. No longer grumpy and hostile like it was earlier. As if the rising darkness has unlocked something in him that he wasn't ready to show before.

His fingers move forward, touching my face, my cheek, tracing over my lips.

"You're really beautiful," he murmurs. I smile.

"For a guy?"

"Yep, even for a guy," he replies, and then I feel his lips on mine again.

I immediately return the kiss, letting his lips press firmly against mine and eagerly opening my mouth as this time it's his tongue that invades me.

A gasp escapes me. I feel this tingling sensation in and on my body, everywhere, especially between my legs. I'm hard again, and instinctively, I press myself closer to him, trying to show him how much I want him.

At the same time, I feel Val's fingers on my neck, gently stroking with his thumbs, softly caressing me.

It's like an electric shock running through me from the spot where he's touching me. But I don't dare move, even though my fingers are itching to slide under his hoodie again, to explore more of him underneath.

I sense that he isn't looking for anything more than this right now. An escape from loneliness, a brief retreat from reality – a kiss that lets him forget everything for a moment.

His hands stay at my neck, fingers threading through my hair. I melt into his lips, but this time the kiss is softer, slower. The wild intensity from earlier fades into something tender, almost hesitant, as if he's trying to figure out how this works. The rhythm is gentle, almost hypnotic—something that could last forever.

Chapter 4

When I open my eyes again, darkness has settled in, and everything is silent except for the faint glow from the pier lights. Val leans back slightly, his lips still glistening from our kiss, a questioning look in his eyes.

"Want to do something else?"

I shrug, still not fully back to the here and now. His question surprises me, piques my curiosity. Mentally, I had already braced myself for everything to be over as quickly as it began, just like before. But there's no trace of tension left on Val's face.

"Sure, you planning to show me the nightlife around here?"

He snorts, his lips curling into an irresistible smile.

"Something like that. There's a music festival one town over tonight, you can ride with me on my bike."

I raise an eyebrow in surprise.

"Your bike – you mean your bicycle, right?" That bright red thing I've already seen him on.

He smirks, nodding.

"Yep, just my bicycle and me. I don't have a driver's license."

I look at him, puzzled.

"You don't have one, or you don't have it anymore...?"

He looks at me, caught off guard, as if he didn't expect me to hit the mark so unexpectedly and has no excuse ready.

But he doesn't back away either, doesn't stand up and leave me hanging.

"The latter," he murmurs quietly, and there it is again, that shadow in his eyes, that brief flash of sadness I saw earlier when he talked about Berlin.

"It's a shitty story and not for tonight."

I can hear in his voice how deep that wound still is. Whatever happened there, in Berlin, it left scars – deep scars. It changed him.

And I fear he won't talk about it now or later. Maybe never.

But I don't have the right to dig into his past. We've only just met. Even though there's a strange magic in this evening and I feel like I've known Val much longer than just a few hours.

"Bike sounds perfect," I say instead. He doesn't respond, just stares off at a point behind me, lost in thought and slightly unsettled.

"Okay..." I murmur, but Val still doesn't react. "Who's playing, what bands?"

That finally seems to snap him out of his thoughts.

"FiveTunes, SLD, the Creeks, and the Harpers," he rattles off quickly.

I stare at him in surprise, not expecting such a detailed answer from him.

"They're all pretty good," he continues, smiling, while I can only stare at him.

Val is a unique surprise package, and damn, the more time I spend with him, the more he fascinates me.

Suddenly, he grins. "What?" he asks.

"Nothing, it's just... you're unbelievably cute right now, and I'm such an idiot for falling hopelessly in love with you" – but I don't say any of that out loud, just keep looking at him like his biggest fan, gasping for breath.

Val's grin grows wider.

Then he starts laughing.

"Shit! How do you do that?" he asks, still chuckling..

"Do what? " I reply innocently, even though I'm laughing too.

I know what he means: his mood, his entire demeanor suddenly seems so light, so carefree. Val isn't the type to just burst out laughing for no reason. And yet, he's doing it – with me.

A contented sigh escapes me, and I can't help myself; I lean forward into his arms and wrap mine around him.

I hear his breath hitch for a moment, but then he gently starts to wrap his arms around my back too. I feel his hand moving, hesitantly, almost tentatively, like I'm neither man nor woman, but some entirely different, yet fascinating creature to him.

I close my eyes briefly, blocking everything out and feeling so complete, so good in this moment with him.

I breathe him in – that hint of salt, sand, and violets clinging to his skin – and nuzzle my face contentedly into the crook of his neck and shoulder. Val lets it happen.

I hear his heartbeat, pounding wildly beneath me, and feel his fingers freeze on my back. Val tenses, then pulls away, making me reluctantly let go.

"It's right by BB's, a restaurant on the beach. They organize it every year." As he talks, he stands up and brushes the sand off his black cargo pants.

Was that too much, too forward on my part?

Val doesn't just shake the sand off his pants; the next time he looks at me, that cool, unreadable expression is back, and the cold blue in his eyes is icy again.

"Bet it's your kind of vibe, city boy – like the city, but with a beach and way more laid-back people." His voice has that frosty edge again.

"Okay..." I murmur, knowing he's trying to tease me. But I won't let him get to me. Not anymore. What he's showing me now is just a façade, and I've caught a glimpse beneath it, under his icy shell. I know there's so much more hidden there than just this coldness.

Val looks down at me, waiting, now also visibly impatient.

"Or do you want to freeze out here?" He winks at me, then, to my surprise, stretches out his hand.

*

A short while later, I find myself on Val's red bike – sitting on the handlebars. It's a completely new and terrifying experience. I hope Val hasn't smoked so much that we end up tumbling off the dike he's speeding along at breakneck speed. Even though Val's arms are wrapped protectively around me, it's a shaky ride.

"Is it far?" I ask in a panic as Val gets dangerously close to the edge of the dike again. He laughs, slows down a bit, and I can feel his breath warm against my cheek. Instantly, I feel calmer and instinctively press my cheek against his. He doesn't pull away, nudging my cheek briefly with his nose. We're so close; it feels good. The fear of falling fades, the panic disappears – his warm skin against mine is all I can think about. His lips lightly brush against my chin, and it's like a lightning bolt hits me, tingling all over and deep inside.

But the moment of closeness between us is far too short. Barely two minutes later, we arrive at a sprawling beach, where a restaurant stands next to a massive stage. Multicolored lights flicker in the distance, and the bass thumps through the air, even from here. I clamber off the bike, my legs stiff and shaky.

Val laughs and winks.

"Was that your first time?"

I look at him, indignant. I hope he's not making an innuendo.

"Yep, and I'd never do something that stupid again voluntarily!" I hiss.

Val steps closer, casually ruffling my hair. That simple, effortless gesture sends my heart racing all over again. I can't help but stare, mesmerized by the blue of his eyes and his lips, still slightly swollen from our kisses. How I'd love to glide my mouth over them again and taste him.

Val grins, tilting his head toward me, and for a moment, I hope he's thinking the same thing I am.

"How're you planning to get back?" he whispers, his lips close enough to brush mine.

I snort. "I'll walk. Seems like a warm night."

He laughs, leaning back. "No way. I've gotta be back by midnight, or my old man will kill me."

"That sounds rough with him," I say, trying to sound sympathetic, noticing Val's muscles tense up.

"He's a total asshole." He crosses his arms.

"Yeah, seems like it."

Val looks away, out toward the beach. "So, you in?"

I glance at him, catching his profile.

Honestly, I'd rather kiss him again. The feel of his lips is addictive. But now, with all these people around us, I doubt we'll get that close once we head toward the stage.

Val doesn't seem nearly as eager as I am. He hasn't even tried to get under my t-shirt or push things further than kissing. It's both frustrating and thrilling. I'm practically melting with impatience standing next to him.

I have no choice but to hold myself together and hope we get some time later to pick up where we left off.

The music pulsing toward us is pretty rock-heavy, sending a shiver through me and making me tap my feet to the beat. It sounds way better than I expected.

I stay behind Val as he carves a path through the crowd and eventually disappears to the side of the stage. I lose sight of him for a moment among all the people but then spot him reappearing next to a blond guy behind a mixing board, greeting him with a handshake.

They dive straight into a conversation, and Val's eyes are fixed entirely on his friend. I wait, but he doesn't glance back at me even once. Sighing, I turn away.

I'm not about to settle for being his shadow tonight. I've got some money with me, so I head over to the wooden bar beneath the stilted restaurant. Maybe tonight I'll get lucky and find a bartender willing to sell me something stronger.

*

I grin at the green umbrella nestled between juicy lime wedges in my glass of bright, ice-cold liquid. I take a sip, closing my eyes in bliss. It's been too long. The sweet-tart flavor swirls on my tongue, and I take another deep gulp.

I glance back at the cute brunette bartender who can't be much older than me. He grins knowingly at me. Yeah, I can enjoy the night here even without the moody blue-haired guy.

Suddenly, I hear someone calling my name and turn around, startled. *Maddie?* I think in surprise. The girl from the kiteboarding course, with her golden blonde hair, is standing right in front of me, grinning excitedly.

"God, I'm so glad to see you here!" she squeals, throwing her arms around me.

"Fuck, me too!" I laugh, hugging her tight.

Maddie pulls back and scans the area.

"Are you here with your family?"

I shake my head, instantly regretting it. That'll just lead to more questions.

"No?" She grimaces. "Lucky you! I had to watch my little sister until just now. They're finally off eating something."

"Cool," I reply with a smile, and at that moment, I spot Val's blue hair again. He's no longer near the stage but chatting with a group not far from here. They all seem to be around his age, and judging by their laughter, they've known each other for a while. A blonde casually runs her hand down Val's back as she whispers something in his ear. A deep, sharp pang shoots through my chest. I quickly turn back to my kiteboarding friend.

"So, who are you here with?" she asks, pressing on.

Maddie is proudly holding a Caipirinha, just like me. We're the same age and have often talked about how hard it is to get alcohol around here.

I take a few deep sips before coming up with an answer she might believe.

"With a friend," I say vaguely.

"From the kite course?"

"No, I met him a few days ago at the Wild Rooster."

"Ah, cool. So, where is he now?"

I shrug.

"Somewhere," I say with a sigh, trying not to glance in Val's direction again.

She starts laughing, and there's this adorable dimple on her right cheek. Honestly, everything about her is charming, young, sweet, almost fairy-like. I really like her.

We've spent a lot of time together in the course. Maddie was one of the reasons I wasn't constantly thinking about Val.

"Well, if you've been ditched, then let's dance! We need to make the most of every minute of freedom!" She purses her lips, tilts her head, and then beams as she looks toward the stage. I can faintly recognize the melody of "Otherside" by the Red Hot Chili Peppers.

Once you know you can never go back
I gotta take it on the other side

Why not? I down the rest of my cocktail in a few quick gulps, feeling the warmth spread through me. Maddie does the same, a playful glint in her eyes as we push our way through the crowd toward the stage.

The music hits me hard, the bass vibrating through my body. The band isn't half-bad, the singer managing to nail the chorus well enough to keep the crowd alive. Not perfect, but good enough for the night.

The alcohol kicks in, making everything feel lighter, sharper, more intense. My cheeks flush, and a tingle spreads through my limbs. Val can go to hell, I think, feeling that lightness replace the frustration.

Maddie moves closer, her body swaying to the rhythm, her eyes half-closed as she loses herself in the music. There's something in the way she looks at me—a softness that lingers, but I push the thought aside. It's just Maddie.

I grab her hand, pulling her closer until we're practically dancing as one. Her arm slips over my shoulder, and her hips press against mine in time with the beat. She leans in, her cheek brushing against mine, and I catch the faint scent of her perfume—something sweet and familiar.

Her fingers linger a little longer on my chest when she spins away, but she's back in an instant, pulling me back into her orbit. I laugh, the sound blending with hers, and for a moment, the world around us fades away. Just Maddie and me, caught up in the music, moving together like we've done this a thousand times before.

There's an ease between us, but there's something else too—something just beneath the surface that I can't quite put my finger on. Her gaze flickers up to mine, but then she grins, her hand squeezing mine as she spins back into me. It's just us, just this moment. And for once, I'm not thinking about anything else. Just this.

Chapter 5

We dance through three more songs—a wild mix of The Offspring, Red Hot Chili Peppers, and Oasis—until thirst drives us back to the bar, where I suddenly spot Val.

This time, he's looking right at me. My first instinct is to wave, but I stop myself and play it cool, sneaking glances in his direction..

Maddie keeps chatting beside me, but once Val's in my line of sight, I can't focus on anything else. It's rude, I know, but the way he's looking at me pulls me back under his spell.

When he finally reaches us, he doesn't say a word, just glances at me before turning to Maddie.

"Val," he murmurs, offering her a quick handshake with a brief, almost surprising attempt at a smile. But I catch a flicker of confusion in his eyes.

"Oh, hi!"

I see her light up again, eagerly shaking his hand, then looking to me with an inquisitive expression. Who's this?, she seems to ask, clearly intrigued.

"You two look wiped out," Val comments.

Maddie grins. "Yeah, we really went all out!" She glances longingly toward the bar, then back at me.

"Another drink?" I ask, giving her a wink.

"Nah, I think my parents are around here somewhere, looking for me. I can't risk getting caught with something strong. See you tomorrow at the course?"

"Absolutely!" I answer with a nod. Maddie giggles and hugs me tightly. I feel her delicate body and her small breasts pressed against me.

Behind me, I hear someone calling her name, and then a man in his mid-forties appears, casting disapproving looks at Maddie, me, and finally Val. Maddie rolls her eyes.

"Well then," she mutters, "have fun, guys. I'm off back to hell."

I smirk and nod. With an exaggeratedly sad face, she turns and follows her father, who throws another reproachful look my way.

As soon as Maddie's gone, Val steps closer.

"I'll grab you some water."

"Or a cocktail?" I try my luck.

Unfortunately, the bartender has changed—this one's way older, and I know my chances of scoring another drink have pretty much vanished.

"Water's probably better for you. You're practically glowing!"

"Nonsense! Besides, how would you know if you haven't even touched me?" I tease, half-serious, half-joking, because I just can't resist.

Val narrows his eyes.

"I saw you in the crowd." He squints at me for a moment.

I grin. "And?"

He crosses his arms, clearly unimpressed.

"What do you mean, 'and'? You were dancing pretty close with her."

I laugh. "Yeah, I was."

He rolls his eyes. Is that... jealousy I hear?

But I don't get a chance to tease him about it. Val heads straight for the bar without another word, and I quickly fall into step behind him.

He glances back at me while we're waiting in line. "There's a way better band coming on soon," he says. "Local group—they play their own stuff. I'm probably gonna produce their first album."

"Oh, cool. So, we're watching them together?" I can't help but grin, and Val lets out a sigh before giving in with a reluctant, "Fine."

He grabs himself a Coke and hands me a bottle of water, which I take with an exaggerated eye roll. But at least he stays by my side.

We move closer to the stage, though the crowd has thinned out after the last band, leaving plenty of space.

Everyone will see us together, know we're more than just friends... The thought makes my heart race. It feels right. As the band starts playing, his arm brushes against mine, his fingers lightly grazing mine.

I can't stop my gaze from drifting to his chiseled profile, watching as he absorbs every note, his head gently nodding to the beat.

Even though I'm barely taking in the music, I can tell Val's right – the band is good, and the lead singer's voice is distinct and beautifully raspy. I can recognize their talent, even in this haze of thoughts centered around Val.

At one point, I dare to take the initiative, brushing my hand across the small of Val's back, like the blonde girl did earlier. He immediately stiffens and shoots me a warning look.

I would love to grab his hand, pull him close, inhale his scent, taste his lips on mine again. But Val doesn't do anything like that; instead, he inches away from me.

It's only when the last notes fade that he turns to me again.

"I'm going to chat with the guys in the band for a bit. You coming along – and keeping your hands to yourself?"

I swallow.

I wasn't even that touchy.

"Hard to say," I grumble, feeling a bit defiant. Val lets out a sigh that's as cold and annoyed as ever. That sharp, standoffish façade is back, instantly crushing any hope I had of something more happening between us tonight.

The truth stings, and for a second, I just want to turn around and leave.

Val heads toward the stage, and I stay put, watching him with frustration bubbling up inside me.

What am I even doing here? Why does this guy—this near-stranger—have such a hold on me?

I'm not his lapdog, someone he can just boss around. Instead of following him, I grab two beers at the bar and head toward the beach, collapsing into an open beach chair with a groan.

Out here, the music is barely a whisper, and I lose myself staring at the stars and the full moon above. There are still 11 days left. Eleven days I've got to somehow survive.

I should've gotten Maddie's number—we could've hung out again. She's so much easier to be around than Val, who's like some icy northerner. Everything feels lighter around her. But Val? That guy is a whole other story. Moody and impossible.

Suddenly, Finn pops into my head—his easy smile, his warmth, his kind brown eyes. I miss him more than I thought I could.

It wasn't love between us, more like a crush. It never burned like this. I never longed for him the way I already do for Val, and I've barely spent any time with him.

Maybe Finn and I were just too young. He's a great guy—good-looking, always kind, never demanding, never stringing me along. But... it just wasn't enough.

Maybe I'm too picky. Maybe I expect too much. Val, though—he's clearly not worth waiting around for.

He's an idiot, doesn't appreciate me. To him, this is nothing. It's not going anywhere.

I'm just an experiment to him. He talked about women who asked him out. He probably ended up in bed with some of them, was probably more direct with them, didn't push their hand away when they touched his back, like he did with the blonde. Maybe she was even one of the women who got really close to Val.

Sighing, I stand up, kick off my shoes and socks, and wade into the water, letting the cool waves wash over my feet and calves.

I tilt my head back, staring at the night sky.

Maybe I should call Finn, text him. Things were so much easier with him. He never had a problem holding my hand, never hid me.

We went out in my hometown, holding hands, kissing in front of everyone. No one cared.

"Thinking of going for a swim?" I hear someone call from behind me. I turn and see Val's icy blue eyes.

Surprised, I freeze, a flicker of hope sparking inside me. But it fades just as quickly when I notice he's not alone. Three guys stand behind him, sizing me up. One of them casually holds a joint between his fingers.

I look back at the sea, not in the mood for him or his buddies. I just want to be alone and wallow in my gloomy thoughts – finally close the chapter on this ice block and leave it all behind.

Chapter 6

Val either doesn't notice my foul mood—which is entirely his fault—or he's deliberately ignoring it. Who knows.

He stands beside me, sipping his beer. I stay silent. So does he. Maybe if I keep ignoring him, he'll just take the hint and leave.

"We're making a fire," he finally says. I sluggishly turn around, glaring at him. Not far behind him, the other three guys are still standing around. They're watching me expectantly. None of them look particularly sober, and Val's gaze is a bit glassy too – probably from the weed or the beer.

"Hey, I'm Cas," I say curtly to the strangers, who sluggishly throw their names back at me: Mark, David, and Karl.

"Come on!" Val says, flashing an unfortunately irresistible smile.

Sighing, I trudge toward the group and only now realize they're the band Val and I watched earlier. David, who I think is the lead singer, wordlessly hands me the joint as I join them.

At least there's that. Gratefully, I take it, inhale deeply, and almost choke. Definitely not the same quality as Val's weed. This stuff is way stronger.

When I go for a third hit, though, Val snatches the joint from my hand.

"Take it easy!" he scolds.

Idiot. The biting retort is on the tip of my tongue, but I swallow it back. I just don't get him – not at all. Why does he even care if I get totally wasted or smoke until I pass out? It shouldn't matter to him. He barely knows me, and he's clearly not interested in me, as he's made painfully obvious over the past few hours.

I just roll my eyes, saying nothing more.

Val and the other two guys soon wander off to gather driftwood for the fire.

David turns to me with a grin. "God, Val's been driving us crazy."

I look at him, confused. "Why?"

"Because of you. Val's been looking for you everywhere." I freeze, staring at David. "Seriously?" I ask quietly, hesitantly, my heart skipping a beat as that stupid flicker of hope reignites.

David nods. "Yep, he said you're his cousin from Bonn, right?"

"He said that crap?" I want to shout, but instead, I clamp my lips shut and don't respond.

"He said you wouldn't be able to get back without him and that he's supposed to keep an eye on you because of his uncle or something like that."

Right... I scuff at some shells on the ground with my foot.

What am I even supposed to say to that nonsense? His ridiculous story about me being his little cousin from the city who needs looking after. I've rarely heard anything more absurd.

"Okay…" the singer mutters, and I can feel his eyes on me, full of questions.
"We were planning to hang out, make a fire, smoke a bit—are you in?"

"Looks like it," I mutter, stuffing my hands into my jeans pockets. I know I didn't sound all that friendly, but I'm not in the mood to pretend or go along with Val's dumb made-up story. David doesn't seem fazed by it, though.

He's actually really nice but also annoyingly curious. As we follow the other guys at a distance, he keeps asking me nonstop about my hometown and my life. I don't give much away, but he doesn't stop talking or questioning me. Maybe he finds what little I do share interesting enough, or maybe it's just because I live in a city with more than a few hundred inhabitants.

Eventually, we're all gathered around a decent-sized campfire, and I find myself staring into the flames. Val isn't beside me; he's sitting across from me. David's on my right, softly strumming his guitar and humming a tune to himself. A joint is passed around again, and despite Val's warning glance, I take more than three hits.

Stop acting like you're in charge, I thought when I took the hits. But now, I'm beginning to understand what that look was about – or at least trying to. My head is a mess, my limbs feel numb, and I can only sit there, hypnotized by the fire. This stuff is really strong. Way stronger than anything I've had before. I don't know how long I sat there, just listening to David's rough, beautiful voice and staring into the flames.

At some point, I snap out of it, hearing the guys burst out laughing. Mark is giggling, talking about a gig they played in a nearby village that was apparently a total flop. The audience consisted of just three people – the waitress, the cook, and his girlfriend. He starts laughing again, and so do David and Karl – but not Val.

Val is looking at me seriously. In his gaze, there's… I don't know, concern? No, more like curiosity.

A tingling sensation washes over me, so intense that it takes all my effort to stay still.

I can feel the weed working through my body in a completely different way than ever before – more intensely than I've ever experienced. It's driving all the blood straight to one place – between my legs – and I feel myself getting harder.

I clench my teeth, trying to snap out of this lust, but it's no use; it's overwhelming me.

I shift subtly, moving my legs, bouncing my foot, but I can only think about how fucking horny I am and how I want nothing more than to hold that throbbing pleasure between my legs in my hands.

A flash of light shoots through my mind: Val kissing me, pulling me close, wrapping his arms around me, sliding his fingers under my clothes, and finally touching me, wanting all of me.

I keep moving, rubbing my erection against the tight fabric of my boxers. It doesn't help – it only makes it worse. I feel precum leaking out, my hardness pressing painfully against my jeans.

A whimper escapes me, and I snap my eyes open, looking around. But the guys are just goofing off, throwing shells and sand at each other, paying no attention to me – except for Val, who keeps glancing my way.

When he catches me looking back at him, he doesn't look away. Instead, he raises one eyebrow, doubtfully. God, he can see it – he knows what's happening to me, knows how much I want him. Shit, I'm burning with desire, even though he's such an asshole.

Sweat starts beading on my skin; I'm burning up. Longingly, I glance at the sea, craving the cool water, wanting to dive in and put out this fire raging inside me.

I look at Val, pleadingly. Why is he sitting so far away? Why isn't he next to me? I'd touch him, slide my hand under his t-shirt, press my face against his neck.

My mind is screaming a warning. No, damn it, this isn't going to happen – not anymore! But it doesn't change this deep desire inside me. I feel like I'm about to explode – right in my jeans.

I can't take it anymore; I'm so hard that either I'm jumping into the sea or getting Val to drag me behind a dune and jerk me off. Shit.

My head and body are just a tangled web of lust and longing.

I'm on my feet, standing upright, before I even fully realize what I'm about to do.

"I'm going swimming," I mumble, stumbling toward the water.

The dark sea sparkles temptingly in front of me, whispering to me with foamy waves: Dive deep into me. I keep walking, heading for the waves. But just before I can dip my feet into the icy water, I feel a strong hand grip my wrist, pulling me back.

"Fuck, what are you doing?" Val's voice is laced with panic as he stares at me. A frustrated huff escapes me. I'm so done with him playing the protector.

I shake him off and start fumbling with my hoodie and then the shirt underneath.

I'm burning up! I tug at my belt, nearly tripping over my own feet.

"Hey Cas, come on! Stop it!" His voice is tense now, genuinely worried. And the look on his face reflects that too.

I burst into giggles, nearly doubling over. What a sight I must be for him! Bet he didn't expect to see this much skin tonight.

"Leave me alone. I need to cool down – I'm so hot!" I manage a few steps, feeling the waves soak through my sneakers. I start to fall forward, nearly landing in the water, when suddenly Val's strong arms wrap around my waist, pulling me back and saving me from the freezing surf.

A jolt of electricity runs through me. I let out a contented sigh, leaning back into him, pressing my cheek against his neck.

"I want you so bad," I growl, my voice dripping with lust. Val pushes me away, and instantly, everything starts spinning around me.

"I'm taking you home," he says sternly. I start laughing again.

"Sure! Go ahead!" I reply way too loudly.

"There's barely any room in my bed, and we'll have to be super quiet!" I say, spinning around and running my fingers over the thin t-shirt he's wearing. I can feel the warmth of his skin underneath, the muscles in his abdomen, the twitch there. I move my hand higher, to his chest, his nipples, feeling the piercing hidden beneath.

"God, you're so hot," I murmur, a mix of a moan and a gasp that's way too loud.

"Can I bite that?" I purr.

"Casper, damn it! Get a grip!" Val snaps, looking at me with a mix of reprimand and near panic. I grin widely, not even bothering to hide it.

I glance over at the fire and sure enough, Mark, David, and Karl are watching us – or rather, watching me. I raise a hand, waving and laughing. I can't quite make out their expressions in the dark, but they're too far away for me to care anyway.

"Everything okay over there?" Mark shouts.

Val waves his arms around, signaling something that seems to say, *I've got this under control.*

Then he turns back to me.

"Come on." Val grabs me around the waist and picks up my discarded clothes as we start walking.

"And fuck, put your t-shirt back on," he growls.

Embarrassed, I nod and do as he says. Then I feel his hand on my wrist again, pulling me along.

Chapter 7

I let myself be dragged along, each step a slog through wet sand in my soaked sneakers. It's exhausting, irritating, and all I want is to collapse into the warm sand and lose myself in Val in the darkness of the night.

"Let's go back to that beach chair and make out," I giggle, suggesting.

Val responds with a sound somewhere between a sigh and a growl—I can't quite tell which.

I'm still dizzy, and my brain can barely form a coherent thought.

"God, I knew this was a mistake," Val mutters, more to himself than to me.

I glare at him, offended. "To meet me or kiss me?"

He shoots me an annoyed look. "Both."

I snort in disbelief. "Wow." Then I take a deep breath, and the fog in my head clears a bit. "Worst date you've ever had, huh?"

"No contest," he sighs.

I roll my eyes. "You really don't know what you're missing out on," I grumble.

"God, Casper, just shut up, okay? We still have a long walk ahead of us, and I have no idea how I'm even going to get you onto my bike in this state."

A sudden wave of self-pity washes over me. What am I even doing here? And why the hell did I smoke so much? Val hasn't exactly seen me at my best tonight.

"Do you hate me now?"

"Don't be stupid – of course not."

"But you don't like me either..."

I stop, staring out at the sea. The campfire is just a faint dot in the distance now, farther away than I realized.

My head is gradually clearing, but my body is still in total turmoil. I can't tell anymore if it's the weed or Val's presence. It's like my hormones go haywire around him. I'm still hard. Even the cold and Val's stupid comments haven't changed that.

I don't get it anymore – how I'm losing it over a guy who isn't even bisexual?

With Finn, I went on several dates before I even wanted to kiss him. I definitely wasn't this desperate, trying to hook up right away.

With Val, I saw him from behind just once in *The Wild Rooster* and immediately wanted to have sex with him. Fuck.

I take a deep breath and keep trudging through the sand. I'm starting to get cold now, the wetness from my feet creeping up my legs.

Val has stopped and is looking at me with concern.

"Sorry," he says unexpectedly when I catch up to him.

I look at him, puzzled, then shrug. Talking seems pointless at this stage – we're just too different, we'll never be on the same page.

Val doesn't move, still looking at me.

"That thing between us wasn't a mistake," he sighs. "I just should've kept you away from that damn weed..."

"It's fine, it's not your fault."

"It is."

I let out a quiet laugh. "Stop trying to act like my protector all the time. I've gotten by just fine on my own." More or less, anyway.

He presses his lips together, then holds out his hand – I guess he's done dragging me around by my hoodie or wrist.

I tilt my head to the side.

"Come on," he says firmly, still holding out his hand.

Sighing, I take it and immediately have to stop. That energy again, surging straight from his fingers into me – that heat. I close my eyes, unable to help myself, and grip his hand tighter.

"Are you okay?" he asks softly.

I open my eyes, staring into that endless blue in front of me.

My brain is still working too slowly, reacting seconds behind everything, and it only realizes what I'm doing after it's already done.

I press myself against Val, crushing my lips to his as I wrap my arms around him.

He stumbles back, cursing softly, caught off guard by my wild kisses, and we both tumble to the ground.

"Ah, damn it!" he hisses.

I can't help but giggle, looking down at him. I'm lying right on top of him, exactly where I've wanted to be this whole time.

"I was just thinking about this," I grin.

He glances up at me. "Do I even want to know what else you've been imagining about me?" I laugh, shaking my head. "Nope, trust me, you don't."

You're something else, Cas!" He sounds half exasperated, half – I can't think about it anymore because suddenly his lips are on mine again, and he's flipping us over, pinning me underneath him.

I let it happen, let him invade my mouth while his hips grind demandingly against mine and his hands finally slide under my sweater. *Fuck yes,* I think, finally!

It's like a foreign force has unleashed my body from all restraints. I'm so uninhibited, so direct, it even scares me – or at least the part of my brain that's still awake.

I say nothing, just press myself against Val, showing him how badly I want him, how crazy I am for him, how much I need him to finally touch me, to use me, to want me.

I moan into his mouth when I feel how hard he's gotten, his impressive length pressing against my jeans and my cock.

Even through the fabric, I can feel him so clearly. I grab at his belt, desperate to feel him naked against me, to have all of him. At the same time, I yank my jeans down, fumbling between us until I've pulled Val's pants down far enough that I'm only feeling the fabric of his tight boxers.

He doesn't stop—he's like an animal now, driven purely by instinct. He grinds against me, kissing me greedily, sucking on my lips, gasping audibly.

I can barely see him in the dark, but I feel every movement—his hips gliding rhythmically against mine. Flashes of light burst behind my eyelids, my whole body tingling, everything pulling me apart.

"Val!" I moan as he licks, nibbles, and sucks roughly at my neck. I run my fingers up and down his torso, finding that promising spot—his nipple with the piercing—and pinch it between my fingers. The reaction is exactly what I was hoping for.

Val gasps loudly, pushing up with his hands, giving me a clear shot. My lips immediately replace my fingers. I suck on his nipple, taking the piercing between my teeth, and feel Val's body trembling above me. He's into it—the pain, the pulling, the biting.

"Fuck, Cas!" he groans, moaning loudly as I suck hard on his nipple and piercing while my hand runs over the fabric, feeling his rock-hard cock beneath.

"Beach chair!" he gasps, stumbling to his feet and staggering a bit. I struggle to keep up, trying not to lose him in the darkness. But it's only a few meters. Val collapses into the chair, and I'm immediately on top of him again, covering his face with desperate kisses, pressing my arousal against him.

My jeans end up discarded in the sand, and Val's stripped down to his boxers. I push his t-shirt up, yanking it off, and my fingers immediately find his nipples again. Val leans into me, letting go, our kisses turning frantic as desire takes over completely.

A shiver of pleasure runs through me. Val presses tightly against me, and I do the same, rubbing my cock against his.

Damn. Dry humping has never felt this good – too good. I press my forehead against his, groaning loudly, feeling all control slipping away.

“Fuck!” I murmur. Val holds me in place as I grind against him, faster and more desperately, like an animal. His fingers slide lower, slipping under my boxers, grabbing my ass. I can't take it anymore – not for another second! No one has ever made me feel this good, not Finn, not anyone, *ever!*

Only Val triggers this volcanic eruption inside me. I know I’m way too loud, moaning, gasping, whimpering under his touch. His fingers sear into my flesh, feeling so insanely good. Especially as they start inching closer to my most sensitive spot.

“Val!” I gasp, capturing his lips one more time, sucking on them as I cum – shit, I cum like a volcano, right into my damn shorts. I can only feel the pleasure coursing through me, the bright light filling me up. I can’t hold it back, can’t control it, just let out everything that’s built up so massively over the past hours.

I don’t know how long I’ve been writhing on top of him, moaning and whimpering, whispering his name, but when I finally open my eyes and look at him, everything is quiet. Val is quiet, completely.

He’s staring at me with wide eyes, his mouth slightly open. There’s astonishment in his gaze.

Fuck, did he… did he not cum?

“Did you just cum in your pants?” he asks, giving me a skeptical look.

I can only nod, and immediately, a heavy feeling settles over me, creeping out from deep within. Shame, doubt, regret – for letting things go this far.

My legs feel like jelly, barely holding me up—but I manage to push myself off him, grab my jeans, and stumble toward the ocean. I can feel the sweat and sand covering almost every part of my body, as well as the sticky wetness of my cum dripping down my inner thighs. God, I feel so dirty, so gross and sticky.

I yank down my boxers and toss them into the waves. Embarrassing. Just flat-out embarrassing.

Then I pull my jeans back on, fix my hoodie and hair, and manage to return to the beach chair, somewhat put together. Val is now standing up too, fully dressed again, but he's still giving me that strange look.

I don't want him to say anything, to comment on what just happened. I can't deal with that right now. I've just bared everything to him after this bizarre date, showing him all of me, my deepest, rawest self – and now... now there's only this painful emptiness inside, knowing I've gone way too far.

Val will never, ever feel anything even close to what I feel for him. And that knowledge hurts like hell.

"I need to go home," I mutter. Val opens his mouth to say something, but I cut him off quickly.

"I'll call a taxi."

With that, I head up from the beach as fast as I can, toward the lights on the pier and the restaurant that point me toward an escape route from this humiliating night.

Chapter 8

I don't want to get up anymore; I just want to lie here, pull the blanket over my head, and block out everything around me. My sisters, who are loudly fighting over their shared tablet at breakfast as if it's a matter of life and death, and my parents, who are discussing the day's plans at the same time.

I hope they think I'm still asleep, praying they didn't notice anything from last night and were already asleep when I finally collapsed into bed, exhausted and full of pain and sorrow. Hopefully, they'll leave the camper soon, and I can take a shower, finally wash away all the shame from my body and feel a little better afterward.

"Cas, sweetheart? " My mom's voice cuts in at the worst possible moment.

I grumble from under the covers, irritated.

"Are you coming with us today? We're finally going to take the ferry to the small island. It'll be nice—there's a huge sandy beach there."

I'm almost tempted to say yes. It's far enough away that Val won't be able to see me, and I won't accidentally run into him. But then it hits my groggy brain that today is also the last kite surfing session, and I promised Maddie I'd be there. And there definitely won't be any Val there. Plus, it's far more appealing than spending the whole day with my family.

"I'm going kite surfing today," I grumble from under the blanket.

I hear my mom get up, walk through the camper, and suddenly sit down on the edge of my bed without warning.

"Don't!" I cry out in alarm. I'm scared she'll smell the mess I got myself into last night just from the bed sheets.

"Where were you last night?" Her tone becomes stricter.

She tugs at the sheet, and I cling to it desperately. I'm still wearing the jeans and clothes from yesterday. And I'm sure it's not the only thing that gives away what happened last night. Memories of Val's bites and sucking on my neck come flooding back. Instinctively, I pull the blanket even further over my head.

"Please, Mom! Just let me sleep!" It sounds more like pleading than asking.

"Get up," she demands. "Right now!"

"Soon," I try, but by then she's already managed to yank the blanket away from me.

Her expression wavers between surprised and confused. I must look like absolute trash.

"Where were you last night?" Now she sounds distinctly alarmed, glancing briefly over at my dad.

I hear him quietly talking to my sisters, who, not three seconds later, leave the camper in loud protest.

Now my dad joins in and looks at me seriously. No idea if he's figured me out as quickly as Mom has.

"Have you looked in the mirror, yet?" he asks, sounding pretty horrified.

I bite my lower lip.

"I just woke up, for God's sake, let me shower first!" I curse. "Then I can tell you..." I trail off.

I don't want to talk to my parents about last night, especially not about that. We've never done that, not like this. They know nothing about Finn. Sure, they knew him, but only as a friend who regularly came over and even stayed the night. They probably never thought about why he suddenly stopped coming over—or did they?

My mom nods.

"But please shower here in the camper," she says softly and then gets up. I must look awful if they don't even want our camping neighbors to see me.

The glance in the mirror reveals the worst. No wonder my parents panicked. My entire neck is red and covered with several hickeys. My lips are badly swollen, and my hair is sticking out in every direction. And to top it off, I feel like every inch of my body is covered in sand, and my scent... Shit. Even I can clearly smell how much I stink—like sex.

I strip off my clothes, stuff them into one of the bags my mom left there for wet swimsuits, and swear to myself that I'll wash them today before Mom gets her hands on them.

It takes a while before I've washed away all the sand and everything else, along with my shame, enough to feel somewhat human again.

My dad still looks deeply concerned when I finally open the camper door and face them. By now, all the windows inside are open. Embarrassing doesn't even begin to cover it.

Still, they come back in, and together we sit down at the table.

My mom pours me some coffee and hands me a bottle of sparkling water, which I greedily drink half of before setting it down again.

“You really don’t need to worry,” I finally say.

“Casper.” My dad only uses my full name when I’m really in big trouble, like with Charlie back then.

“I know, almost 17, you don’t want us constantly making rules for you or interfering in your private life, but...” He trails off, shaking his head. God, it really sounds like it did back then with Charlie, damn it.

“I’m fine, really! Nothing happened!” I insist again.

My mom sighs.

“You met someone last night.” Her gaze pierces me. “And don’t deny it now!”

I take a deep breath.

“Well, yeah...,” I grudgingly admit, “but it wasn’t anything serious, okay? I don’t get why you’re both acting so weird about it.”

"The fact that it wasn’t serious, ” my mom says, putting air quotes around ‘serious,’ "makes it even worse for us!”

Suddenly, the strictness in her voice fades, and her eyes grow wide with concern. "Damn it, Cas..." she sighs, lightly brushing her fingers over mine. "What are you doing?" I can clearly hear the tremble in her voice. Shit. They’re genuinely worried.

I close my eyes briefly while my dad continues speaking.

"I don’t even know where to begin," he groans, sounding utterly helpless. "And yes, I know this is uncomfortable for you right now, but we can’t just stay out of it anymore and continue to give you so much freedom here when you’re putting yourself in such danger!"

Stunned, I stare at him. Something’s seriously wrong here.

"Nonsense!" I snap. "I was never in danger!"

My dad crosses his arms over his chest.

"Casper," he repeats in that relentless tone. "Your eyes are bloodshot, your lips are swollen, your neck is covered in marks and... and your smell this morning..." He shakes his head in disbelief at his own words, and I wish a deep hole would open up in front of me and simply swallow me.

"Dad!" I yell out in protest. But he only shrugs helplessly.

"Seriously, didn’t you ever have sex on the beach when you were young?" I groan.

Maybe attacking is the best defense...

My dad lowers his gaze, while my mom looks at him helplessly. There's something they're struggling to say, but they can't seem to get it out.

Suddenly, I'm gripped by an overwhelming fear.

Damn, what did I risk last night? What did I put on the line?

Have they figured it out?

I never wanted to talk to them about it, and that hasn't changed now, but hell, they seem to know something. *No!* I scold myself internally, trying to calm down. My head is just messed up from the leftover alcohol and weed in my blood.

They can't suspect, can't know—how would they have come to that conclusion? They don't know Val, they've never seen me with him before. Desperately, I try to think of a story they might believe, but then my mom continues speaking.

"Cas... we don't have a problem with you exploring your sexuality." She gently strokes the back of my hand again.

Internally, I want to gag at her words. They sound like they're straight out of a dusty old textbook.

"But you must be careful, and you shouldn't meet strangers."

"What the hell are you even implying?" I snarl defensively.

My dad lets out a sigh, taking a deep breath.

"Cas... we know, well... that you're attra— I mean, that you're interested in men..." He trails off, unable to fully articulate it. But his half-finished words are enough to make my heart pound like a jackhammer and a wave of unspeakable anger rise within me.

"Damn it, what's all this crap about?" I curse, standing up abruptly, but immediately, my dad grabs my wrist, looking at me pleadingly.

"Please, Cas, sit back down, we really don't have a problem with it!"

Damn, I don't want to sit back down. My heart is racing in my throat; I just want to get away from here. I never wanted to have this conversation with them—never! It's my private life, damn it! My business alone, who I choose to meet.

"Casper," my mom says in a much softer tone now, trying to smile.

"We're on your side, absolutely, we love you," she assures me.

I look at her in disbelief, already knowing that the big "but" is about to follow. I swallow hard as she finally continues.

"But we are incredibly worried about you right now."

I roll my eyes, and she keeps talking.

"Worried that you're being reckless… that you're not thinking things through." She takes my hand again, but this time, I pull it away. She doesn't give up, though.

"Casper, there are enough men out there who could be truly dangerous to a boy your age."

I scoff disdainfully. What horror novel are they pulling this from?

Suddenly, my dad pulls out my phone and places it on the table. A brief showdown follows between us. I can't believe it. They wouldn't dare snoop through my phone, would they?

"Cas," he continues, confirming all my worst fears a moment later.

"We know you have Grindr on your phone." My dad looks at me, clearly alarmed. "We know you've been to gay clubs and met men…" The accusations hang between us, and I'm too stunned to speak.

For a moment, my heart stops in shock. They really do know—everything! Damn it, just everything!

But what they're accusing me of is absolute bullshit! Completely absurd and has nothing to do with what happened last night!

"What the hell do you think of me?" I hiss. "That I'm hooking up with random guys? That I let anyone have a go if they're up for it?" Now I'm shouting, my voice full of rage—they don't understand a damn thing.

"Fuck it!" I curse, my voice cracking, partly from frustration and partly from disappointment.

"I had a boyfriend until two months ago," I rasp. "And just because I have an app on my phone or go out at night doesn't mean I'm meeting any random idiots!"

My dad raises his hands apologetically. My mom also looks at me with a wounded expression.

"Sweetheart, please calm down, we believe you!"

Sullenly, I slump back into the chair.

"Then stop talking such crap." I let out a frustrated sigh. "I didn't have sex last night, at least not in the way you seem to think, damn it!" I curse, and tears sting my eyes.

"Okay... you just looked—well, it seemed like..." My dad's voice falters, but I can finally sense where all of this is coming from, what's driving their concern. "Like someone had..."

"What, like someone had abused me?" I snarl, now understanding their panic. "Do you really think I'd let that happen?"

"You can't always control it," my mom tries to defend herself.

"God, I'm into guys, yes, but I'm not some kind of fuckboy!" That might have been a bit too blunt and harsh for my parents. They look at me in shock. But I need to, no, I HAVE to clear this up once and for all—that their assumptions are completely off, that I'm not that kind of guy and that I don't put myself in unnecessary danger.

"And yes," I add, a bit more softly. "I did meet someone last night, but it wasn't like that, okay? I met him because it meant more to me than just a damn sex date, is that enough? Or do you want to know more?"

My dad sighs.

"Did you drink alcohol last night?"

He just can't let it go. Frustrated, I close my eyes.

"Did he give you alcohol or drugs?" my mom asks, still sounding worried.

I shake my head, tired. It'd be stupid not to lie right now.

"No! Damn it, can we drop this now?"

Both of my parents press their lips together.

Silence hangs in the air for a moment. I need that time, too—to pull myself together, to process everything.

Finally, my mom speaks again. "While we're here, we want you to check in with us. And if you meet that boy again, you need to tell us, okay?"

"Don't worry," I grumble. "I'm not meeting him again—ever."

My mom's concern flares up again instantly.

"Not because he hurt me, alright? He just doesn't like me," I mumble quietly.

And suddenly, I feel my mom's arms around my back. From worried to affectionate—that shift happened way too fast.

"Don't," I whisper, trying to resist this unexpected closeness, but at the same time, it feels so good. Damn, the child in me craves these brief moments of full attention from my mom, her warm, soft arms around me.

"You are absolutely wonderful, Cas, just the way you are, and I'm sure someone will come into your life soon who sees that too."

"Sure," I mumble into her thick curly hair.

She smiles as she pulls away, and I can't help but smile back. In a strange way, as awful as this conversation was, it's left me feeling calmer.

My parents know now; that wall between us is gone. Only now do I realize how much I've distanced myself from them over the past few years because of it.

My mom doesn't push me to keep talking, doesn't bombard me with questions, but I feel the urge to continue—to finally confide in her.

We used to be so close, and for the first time in a long time, it feels like that again. Feeling her fingers at the nape of my neck brings back that incredible sense of security, and bit by bit, I start opening up to her.

I talk about Finn, show her pictures of us, and that familiar urge rises in me—to write to him, to try again. This time, more seriously.

*

It was already late afternoon when I finally went to the kite school. Today's kite surfing started much later due to the tide. Maddie and I were paired up again, sharing a kite and making really good progress. I even managed to stick a few jumps, and according to the instructor, next time I can rent a kite directly without having to take another course. I never would have thought I'd make it this far, especially not here in Germany.

After the two-hour course, Maddie and I sit together in front of the kite school with a soda in hand, and I've finally been able to shake off all the shame and chaos in my feelings.

I'm sure Val won't contact me anymore. He doesn't even have my number, doesn't know where I live here—it's all good. That's actually quite comforting for me. However, I notice the curious look from my teammate, as if something's on the tip of her tongue and she's about to burst if she doesn't say it soon.

"What?" I ask with a grin.

"You didn't say anything about last night..." She sounds slightly accusatory.

"Well, there's not much to tell," I reply curtly.

"Okay..." Her voice doesn't sound like she believes me.

"Have you been with your friend for long?"

"My friend..." I repeat her words quietly, snorting to myself. The word "friend" can mean anything coming from Maddie's mouth.

I study her briefly, but no, it's impossible that she's figured me out as easily as my parents did.

She looks at me questioningly. "Everything okay?"

"Yeah, I think so."

"Okay... it's really none of my business, Cas, but that guy... the way you looked at him." She swallows. "It kind of seemed like you two..."

Maddie doesn't finish the sentence.

Sighing, I look back at her and take a big gulp of my soda. I don't want to lie to her, nor do I want to keep pretending.

"Yep," I answer bluntly to her unspoken question.

"Okay... sorry, it's our last evening, and I... well, I..." She takes a deep breath.

"I like you, a lot," she whispers, looking away and brushing a long blonde strand out of her face.

I look at her, surprised. At the same time, I can see how hard it must have been for her to get those few words out. Her cheeks are completely red, and she's nervously biting her lower lip. Internally, I curse myself. It would be so easy if I could just lean over and kiss her. The kiss would be sweet and charming, just like her entire personality. But I just can't do it.

"Maddie... damn, I'm sorry..."

"It's okay," she sighs.

"No, it's not. I like you, a lot, but I just... can't..." My voice trails off, the words stuck in my throat.

She nods, giving me a shy smile. "Because you're in love with that boy with the blue hair?"

I press my lips together. "Yeah, but it doesn't matter anymore. He's out of the picture."

"Oh..." She inches a little closer. "If you ever want to talk about it..." she offers softly.

"No," I cut in quickly. "It's better if I just forget about that idiot."

"That bad?"

"Yep," I mutter. It still hurts. Falling head over heels in love and getting nothing but pain and frustration in return. No one, not even Maddie or my parents, can do anything about these bitter feelings. But it'll get better—at least, I hope so.

Around 9 PM, I say goodbye to Maddie at the kite school. I give her one last hug, feeling how perfectly her small frame fits against mine. But just as quickly, the moment slips away. She suddenly stiffens, pulling back and looking up at me, her expression surprised.

"What?" I ask, confused. I can see the questions swimming in her eyes.

"Him." Maddie doesn't need to say more. I already know who she means. Without turning around, I feel a sharp jolt run through my entire body.

I don't dare look back.

Chapter 9

With concern and curiosity in her eyes, Maddie looks at me.

"You should go," I say softly, trying to smile, but it only makes Maddie look at me with even more worry.

"I'm really fine, I promise!" I insist. She nods hesitantly. "Will you text me?"

"Of course!" Maddie gives me one last hug before leaving, and I turn to face my fate. I turn and lock eyes with those ice-blue irises.

That familiar electric jolt hits me again—his gaze is so direct, so intense, I momentarily forget to breathe.

"Valentin." I'm not sure why I say his name so nervously, fully pronounced like that.

"Casper." A small smile tugs at his lips, and I'm caught completely off guard. It throws me off balance.

Is he not angry? Shocked? Why is he even here? Was it coincidence, or did he plan this?

It's only been 24 hours since that disastrous date. Twenty-four hours where my life got flipped upside down, and I tried everything not to think about it—or him.

"What are you doing here?" The words slip out before I can even think.

He flashes that playful grin, and I'm already melting.

"Why not?" he says with a casual shrug.

My whole body stiffens. No way—he's not mad. Not at all.

A far-too-happy and overly hopeful smile spreads across my face.

"Got any time?" he asks, like it's no big deal.

I laugh, shaking my head. "Are you seriously asking me that? You're the one who's always working nonstop!"

He shrugs again. "Told my old man I was taking off some overtime hours." He lets out a dry laugh. "He freaked out, so I bailed."

I grin. "All that trouble just for me?"

He shrugs, giving a small smile. "I think you're worth it." As he says that, his fingers lightly brush against my forearm. My heart flutters wildly, and my thoughts race.

How did everything turn around so quickly? How is Val here, with me? And damn, how could I have misjudged him so badly?

"Wanna take a walk?" he asks quietly, his eyes tracing my face, lingering just a little too long on my lips.

I nod, too stunned to say anything.

We walk away from the stretch of beach where the kite camp is set up. I have no idea where he's leading me. There are still too many people around for anything more, but I'm just happy to be walking beside him, having him here with me again.

After walking in silence for a while, Val suddenly stops and unlocks a beach chair. It's off to the side, away from the crowds of tourists on the beach.

With a sigh, he sinks into the chair and kicks up the footrest. I'm still standing there, in disbelief, watching him. The sun is setting, casting a magical, golden light over Val. He sits there, completely relaxed, his eyes closed, looking so distant, so removed from everything—like he's in a world of his own. He looks like a dream, and I have to pinch myself to believe he's really here, sitting right in front of me.

A quiet, amused huff escapes me when I feel the sting on my wrist. No dream.

"Shit, I kind of thought you'd never want to see me again," I blurt out.

Val blinks up at me against the sun and laughs in that gravelly way that makes everything inside me buzz and tingle. Grinning, he pulls out two Jever beers from his backpack and hands one to me. Hesitantly, I reach for it, afraid that just touching him might shatter everything again.

But Val stays put, even when my hand brushes against his. He smiles, and I dare to sit next to him, still staring at him in disbelief. He blinks at me, and I smirk.

"Why'd you think that?" he asks.

My cheeks heat up as I shrug helplessly.

" Because you lost yourself right there on my lap?" Val says, grinning with no filter, so bluntly that I gasp in shock.

"Shit... *yeah*!" I laugh, taking a few gulps of beer, trying to wash down the rest of my embarrassment. "That was so fucking embarrassing, sorry!"

He tilts his head toward me, squinting slightly. "Did you really just apologize for that?"

I press my lips together.

"I mean..." he murmurs. "It was intense, but at the same time..." He smirks. "It was also really cute, real. You're not putting on a front with me." His hand briefly brushes against mine, and then he adds in a softer tone, "I think that's what I like about you... a lot, actually."

I stare at him in amazement. My stomach is in knots with a whirlwind of emotions, and even my feet start to tingle. Shit, I'm falling for him.

"Seriously?" I manage to get out.

"Yeah." He winks at me. "Even though it took me a few hours to recover after that, just to be able to think straight again..." He laughs softly.

I'm not sure what to say. I went through the same thing.

"You really messed me up, *fuck*!" He takes another swig of beer.

"Wow," I breathe, not sure if he even hears it over the sound of the waves and the screeching seagulls.

But Val takes a deep breath, nods slightly, and leans closer to me. I think he's about to kiss me, but then he pulls back suddenly, gripping his beer bottle tighter.

"Shit, I mean, yeah, damn, I tried." He shakes his head. "Tried to get you out of my head, but I just couldn't."

For a few seconds, everything—my breath, my heartbeat—seems to stop. I look at him, wide-eyed. "Shit, really?"

I tentatively take his hand, and he doesn't pull away. Our fingers intertwine, and we sit in silence, just staring at each other.

The spark I feel from Val's warm skin against mine is undeniable. I want to kiss him so badly, to be as close to him as possible. This heat is burning inside me, but it's not like our date—we're not alone, and it's still too bright out. But none of that lessens the overwhelming desire I feel. It grows stronger with every breath of his intoxicating scent. I press my lips together, turning to look at the sea. Beside me, I hear him sigh in frustration too.

For a moment, my parents' warnings echo in my mind. It's already after 10 p.m. I know I've stayed out too late again, and I'm in for another round of questions and trouble.

But those thoughts fade away when I feel Val's arm wrap around my shoulder, pulling me close, making the burning desire inside me even worse.

No, I can't resist him. I can't hold back anymore. His fingers lightly trace along my neck, feeling the rapid pulse beneath the skin.

I turn my head and look at him. Val is so close, so damn close...

Val. My mind goes quiet, my reason switches off, and I hungrily press my lips to his. Screw what's happening around us—I need to taste him, feel him!

He doesn't pull away, doesn't break the kiss. Instead, he tightens his arms around me, pulling me even closer. Chest to chest, I can feel his body, the life pulsing beneath the surface, his racing heartbeat. And his tongue, that cool piercing sliding over my lips, slipping inside, teasing mine, making me forget everything.

Heat courses through me, and a deep moan escapes me as I feel his fingers slip under my sweater, sliding down to my lower back and slipping under the waistband of my jeans, caressing the curve of my ass. A husky "More" slips from my lips.

I'm so hard, I want him so much! I can't think straight, so I climb onto his lap, but as soon as I settle on his equally hard bulge, he breaks the kiss and looks at me. Breathless, with swollen lips and a fiery gaze.

"Shit, Cas!" he curses, taking deep breaths. I press my forehead to his. We're both burning up, and I can feel the fine sheen of sweat on our skin.

"I want you," I murmur, a mix of whimper and plea escaping me.

"Cas!" he rasps back. His fingers trace up my back, to my nape, pulling me closer again for another kiss. This time with such urgency, such need that I forget to breathe for a second. My fingers slide under his t-shirt, digging into the skin just above his hips. I feel his hips instinctively press forward, into me.

A loud moan escapes me, and I can't stop myself from grinding against him again, pressing my hard-on against his through our clothes. I've learned nothing, absolutely nothing. But any sense of reason drowned with the sun in the sea.

I whimper, moan, sigh, feeling everything inside me tighten and spin as I get dizzy from the kiss and Val's heated body.

But then suddenly, Val's hands are no longer under my sweater but over it, pressing against my chest. Panting, he gently pushes me back, and a regretful, almost pained expression crosses his face.

I see the battle he's fighting to be the reasonable one, how hard it is for him to stop now.

"Let's take a few steps, okay?" His voice is hoarse and raspy, and it sounds incredibly strained.

Everything inside me is screaming 'no,' but I manage a slight nod. Val's right—it can't end like our first date again. I can't, and I shouldn't, risk everything tonight.

I get up from his lap, my legs shaky, and quickly glance around. The beach has mostly emptied out. Only an older couple and a small group of people around our age remain nearby. But even that feels like too many, considering what just happened between us.

The sky above is still a deep blue, not yet black or full of stars—no comforting cover of darkness like last night. As we stand, the older couple's unmistakable looks tell me they noticed us. They heard us.

Val doesn't take my hand as we walk along the beach, and I can't find the words. I don't know what to say, still too overwhelmed by what just happened.

We head toward a wooden pier that stretches out into the sea. When we reach the end, with the waves crashing around us and the darkness setting in, Val stops and stares out at the water.

"I don't know how this can work," Val says quietly. It feels like he's talking more to himself than to me.

When I catch his profile, I can see the internal struggle playing out in his head. I'm not sure if he's grappling with the fact that he's into a guy now or just frustrated with how hard it is for us to find any privacy. He runs a hand over his face, pushing a stubborn blue strand of hair behind his pierced right ear.

And, fuck, I don't get it," he says, shaking his head and turning to look at me, his expression full of questions as if searching my face for answers. I shrug helplessly, unsure of what to say.

Suddenly, his right hand moves forward, cupping my cheek, holding it firmly.

"Why can't I get you out of my head? Why do I react so strongly to you? Fuck, I've never been into guys! Not at all!" His voice is full of frustration and irritation, but it doesn't scare me. Instead, it sends a warm shiver through my stomach.

From the curiosity of our first date, something has grown that neither of us expected. Knowing that he's struggling internally just as much as I am—trying to make sense of it all, trying to understand, organize, and put it into words—makes the warm feeling in my stomach swell even more.

Damn it, I've never been this smitten, never felt so in love! I didn't even know butterflies in the stomach were a real thing—until now. I feel them, and I'm completely captivated by Val. Damn, I know there's no turning back for me, even if I end up being the fool with a broken heart.

Here in the north, during this brief time we have together, everything else fades into the background. I feel an indescribable happiness, but I also know there will be consequences. When I finally return home, Val will be lodged too deeply in my heart—like a thorn that's become embedded, impossible to remove, and I'll suffer like never before. But even knowing this, I can't stop myself from moving forward. I can't sever the unexpected connection that's formed between us. I can't leave Val behind for the sake of my own well-being. It's simply impossible.

He looks at me, as if expecting an answer.

"I have no idea what you want to hear from me," I say with a sigh, stuffing my hands into my jeans pockets. The darkness has now completely taken over. I can barely see my hand in front of my eyes. The black sky and sea have wrapped us in their embrace, thundering loudly around us. Val's hand moves from my cheek to my shoulder, as if he's making sure I haven't been swallowed by the darkness. Instinctively, I press myself against him again, and Val immediately wraps his arms around me, pulling me close. I bury my face in the crook of his neck and shoulder, planting soft kisses on his wildly pulsing artery.

From far away, I hear a bell toll. Eleven times.

My parents pop back into my mind.

I look up at him, frustrated.

"I just know I'm going to get in trouble with my parents again, and we only have 9 days left here to figure this out..." I trail off. Finish it? Understand it? Make it something more? A frustrated sigh escapes me.

"Cas," he murmurs, taking my hand and fumbling with his phone until he finds the flashlight.

"I'll walk you back now."

I nod, and we walk back in silence, the sound of waves crashing beside us.

He doesn't let go of my hand, even when we reach the brightly lit area of the shore.

"I'll take the next few days off, okay?" he says as we approach the entrance to the campsite.

"You're going to get in big trouble," I sigh.

He shrugs.

"So what? My old man can deal with it. Don't worry about it."

I study him for a moment.

"Hey." Val grins, brushing his thumb over my lips. "We'll see each other tomorrow, and I'll think of a way for us to..." He trails off, taking a deep breath.

"To have more than just dry sex?" I grin way too broadly.

"Shit, Cas!" he snorts, and I notice a blush creeping across his cheeks.

"I want you," I repeat my words from earlier and dare to move closer again, pressing my forehead against his and kissing him one last time. It's much more tender, softer. More of a tasting than a devouring. It tastes like the anticipation of tomorrow.

"All of you," I whisper hoarsely as I pull away. My breath, my lips, everything about me is trembling.

For a moment, Val's expression softens, and he looks at me with a kind of wonder.

"Fuck, I want you too," he growls, and once again, it's too much; I'm already hard again, completely out of control and crazy about him.

Val stands close enough for me to read every emotion on his face.

He's no longer the cold, distant boy I first met. His eyes practically glow when he looks at me now. He seems warm and open and, yes, turned on too.

His fingers briefly brush mine, trailing down my jeans, over my hips, barely grazing my crotch, making me let out a soft whimper immediately. He grins knowingly and pulls his hand away.

"You'll just have to hold out until tomorrow," he smirks.

I tilt my head, a teasing challenge in my eyes, and let my hand dart forward, right to his center, making him gasp in surprise.
"So will you," I growl, catching the knowing smirk on his face.

Chapter 10

"So?" My mom's serious gaze pierces me, making my mind race through all the ways I could calm her down. But none of them are solid—just half-baked ideas, nothing she'd actually buy. Nothing real.

"It was barely two hours!" I blurt out, not really as an excuse for being late, more like a weak defense.

"Two hours with no idea where you were, ignoring our messages and calls!" Even my dad, usually the one to calm her down, looks genuinely worried. Not today though—now that they know everything.

I glance helplessly around the camper, spotting my sisters with their earbuds in. I can only hope they're not overhearing this conversation, but knowing them, they're probably just pretending to listen to music.

I want to see Val tomorrow. I don't want to waste another day. But convincing my parents of that? God, it feels impossible right now.

Today was the last day of the kite course, which would've been the perfect excuse to see him, even just for a few hours without them knowing.

The truth seems like my only option, so I sigh, drop into the chair at the table, grab the steaming cup of tea in front of me, and give them a resigned look.

"I met up with him briefly," I mumble.

"Casper!" My mom's tone is sharp.

"What?" I snap back, irritated.

"On the beach, where there are tons of tourists. Is that forbidden now too, or what?"

She closes her eyes briefly, takes a deep breath, and then sits down next to me.

"I'm not trying to stand in your way or keep you from seeing him, Cas," she says softly, gently stroking the back of my hand. "But you're the one who said you wouldn't see him again, and we know absolutely nothing about this boy you're meeting..."

Frustrated, I cross my arms on the table and drop my head onto them.

What can I possibly tell them about Val that won't make them worry even more? The five-year age difference doesn't bother me at all, but I know it'll be a big deal for my parents. And then there's the whole tattoo and piercing thing, which definitely won't do me any favors. Val isn't exactly the type of guy you'd bring home to meet the family—especially with that cold, standoffish vibe he gives off. They'd freak out.

"What is it you wanna know?" I grumble, doubting that any answer I give will actually help me get to see him again.

"Well, let's start simple." She gives me an encouraging smile. "What's his name?"

I glare at her suspiciously. "Val," I reply curtly.

"Val?" My dad echoes.

"Valentin. Happy now?" I roll my eyes.

My mom nods, and I sit up straighter, trying to shake off my nervousness.

"And where did you meet him?"

"Seriously?"

She nods, unfazed by my attitude.

"Does he live here at the campsite or in town?"

"Town!" I snort. Calling this tiny coastal village a town is the exaggeration of the year! But then I quickly pull myself together. That detail doesn't matter. Val lives here, and ever since we met, this place feels a lot less small and boring. Hell, even the weather's been better since our first encounter.

"He lives with his dad, and I met him at the *Wild Rooster*. He works there."

My dad looks at me thoughtfully, then it seems like something clicks in his head.

"Is that the rude guy behind the counter with the blue hair?"

"Dad!" I gasp, shocked that he figured it out so quickly. Why do my parents have to know me so well?

My dad exchanges a glance with my mom, and it's clear they've instantly formed an opinion about him.

"God, he has to work there because his dad owns the restaurant. He's actually really nice!" At least, sometimes...

"So nice that he's not interested in you," my mom fires back. "Those were your words about him, Cas, not mine." She crosses her arms again, looking more worried than ever.

"Damn it, mom!" I shout, but she just keeps giving me that annoying, judgmental look.

I gesture helplessly with my arms. I don't want to talk about Val with them. I don't want to share anything that's only between him and me, but my parents are relentless.

"It's not easy for him either, okay? He's not... shit, he's not really into guys. I think he's pansexual or something. Are you seriously holding that against him? You're always telling me not to judge people before getting to know them, and now you're doing exactly that with him? Without even meeting him?"

My parents exchange guilty looks. Finally, a point for me. But unfortunately, it doesn't last long.

"Then we should probably meet him soon!" my mom suggests, completely serious, and I almost choke on my tea.

"Oh God, come on," I groan. This is the dumbest idea ever.

Val isn't someone you introduce to your parents. The plan was simple: have a good time—including mind-blowing sex—and then go home and move on. This fling has no future; I know that. Why should Val have to prove himself? Why does it have to get so complicated?

"No, Casper." Now it's my dad speaking. "That's the deal. You can see him if we at least meet him once and get a sense of what he's like."

*

I should've just made up a stupid excuse, like claiming the kite course is still going, instead of agreeing to this ridiculous idea of my parents.

We're sitting in the restaurant *BBs,* right above the beach where Val and I made out so passionately. My parents, and even my sisters, are here.

I hate it. I don't want them snooping around in my life. It's none of their business, even less so for my sisters. But any protest I made was immediately shot down. I ran out of time to come up with a new plan.

Val surprised me, though. When I texted him yesterday and asked if he'd be up for briefly meeting my parents, he agreed right away—without even asking many questions.

So here we are, all sitting together at one of the tables in the BB's, right by the window with a stunning view of the sea, waiting—for Val.

Nerves are eating me up inside. I can't drink, can't eat any of the bread on the table, even though I haven't eaten anything since this morning. I'm a bundle of nerves, almost hoping he won't show up and won't put himself through this mess with my family. It's beyond embarrassing and only highlights how young I still am, not even able to leave the house without my parents' permission.

I'm bouncing my leg up and down. The waiter has already come by twice to take our order, but my parents told him we weren't ready since we were still waiting for someone.

"Who are we even waiting for?" Lina, my sister, asks, glancing up from her phone in boredom.

My mom gives her a secretive smile, then shoots me that weird look.

Of course, that catches Larissa's attention too.

"Do you have a girlfriend now or something?" she asks, eyeing me suspiciously. They've both teased me enough in the past for not having a girlfriend, saying it's totally weird for my age.

"Mind your own business, okay?" I snap back, earning a swift kick under the table.

"Casper!" my mom jumps in immediately, while I glare angrily across the table at Larissa.

"What? How much more embarrassing does this have to get?" I hiss.

My dad gives me a warning look.

"It's true! I'm already at rock bottom, and you're all just kicking me while I'm there!"

"No one's kicking you while you're down, sweetheart!"

"Yes, you are! This is just so unnecessary and super embarrassing!"

"Why?" my mom asks calmly. "I think it's important that we meet him." She says it so serenely that I have to bite the inside of my cheek hard to keep from shouting in frustration.

"Him?" my sisters say in unison.

Shit.

A loud, exasperated "Fuck!" escapes me.

"You guys are the worst!" I snap at my parents, completely out of patience. All I want to do is stand up and leave.

My sisters are still staring at me in confusion, but my mom smiles reassuringly at me. And that's when the saloon-style doors of the restaurant swing open, and Val walks in, making everything else disappear from my mind.

His hair is so blue, his eyes so bright, and his whole presence, his aura, sweeps through me like a whirlwind.

I swallow hard and timidly raise my hand, but he's already seen me. Val strides confidently over to us, wearing a slightly too determined, almost smug, and amused smile.

My mother stands up to greet him, as does my father. Only my sisters and I remain seated. They stare at him with questions, the only ones at the table not in the loop. My hands get sweaty.

I watch as Val flashes a charming smile and greets my mom and dad politely. Whether it works, who knows. They're both eyeing his facial piercings and earrings with barely concealed skepticism, not to mention the tattoos visible through his light t-shirt. I press my lips together anxiously. This is never going to work.

Val sits down right next to me, like it's the most natural thing in the world, and gives my sisters a quick nod. They glance at him, surprised but intrigued. Under the table, Val briefly squeezes my hand, and I look at him in surprise.

"Thanks," I whisper. He blinks in a way that says, "It's fine." His knee brushes against mine, and that captivating smile of his sends a shiver down my spine.

I bite hard on my lower lip to stop myself from moaning out loud. It's just too much Val, all at once, and I can barely sit still or think straight.

*

Val is doing surprisingly well. He talks about his time in Berlin, his training as a sound engineer, his plans, and his Firebird, which is parked at a friend's place. He's never mentioned the car to me before. Why he even has it or how he got it without a driver's license is beyond me.

But I'm not about to ask him about it now, in front of my family. I know there must be something significant and painful behind it, and that's none of their business.

As it turned out shortly afterwards, the car belonged to his late grandfather. Val inherited it from him. My dad's eyes light up when he hears that.

He has a garage that specializes in exactly those kinds of American muscle cars. Finally, the ice is broken.

My parents stop their Q&A session and focus on something else—the menu and the food. But my sisters keep sneaking glances at Val. I don't want to know what they're thinking or what they're going to ask me later.

"Should we share something?" Val asks me quietly, leaning so close to my ear that goosebumps form on my neck.

The suggestion—somehow sweet and genuine. Whether it's because he's low on cash or just being thoughtful—it doesn't matter. Sharing something with Val makes the butterflies in my stomach flutter even more, and my knee presses more firmly against his under the table. I grin at him in response. I'm not really hungry anyway.

Even though the food looks good, I mostly just nibble at the antipasti platter we're sharing. Val, on the other hand, seems to be enjoying it, probably a nice change from the home-style cooking at *The Wild Rooster.*

"Cas, you're not eating enough again!" my mom scolds, as expected.

Val grins beside me, sliding his hand up my thigh under the table, making me let out a quiet gasp. "Just one more bite, sweetie, or you'll be out of energy later," he teases with a smirk. I nearly choke, praying my family didn't catch that.

I shoot him a warning look, but I can't stop the blush from creeping up my cheeks.

After an hour of small talk about the area and the nearby islands, I finally gather the courage to squeeze Val's hand under the table and stand up.

"We're going to head out," I say, a bit abruptly.

Val glances up at me, then stands as well. I turn to my parents, hoping for their approval. My mom sighs, but my dad nods.

"Be back by 10 PM at the latest!"

"Dad!" I protest, but Val's hand gently brushes against my back, finding mine and giving it a reassuring squeeze. A smile spreads across my face. He's right—even in just two hours, a lot can happen.

Chapter 11

We walk side by side in comfortable silence, our hands occasionally brushing. Neither of us pulls away, playing along with this quiet, unspoken game. I grin, and Val mirrors it. Inside, I'm buzzing with excitement. Everything with my parents earlier was crazy—but that's all behind us now.

Suddenly, I start laughing, first softly, then louder until it bursts out uncontrollably. Val glances at me and then breaks into laughter himself.

"Damn, you're crazy," he says, still laughing, his whole body shaking. I pause, watching him. In his bright eyes and wide grin, there's a lightness I never could've imagined just days ago.

"Maybe," I reply, grinning. Then I bump my shoulder against his, and we start roughhousing, grabbing and shoving each other until we're both laughing and lying in the sand.

I feel Val's weight on me and the warm sand beneath me. The sun hangs low on the horizon, painting the sky in a glowing mix of warm orange and soft pink. I can feel his heartbeat pounding against my chest, and my lungs fill with the salty sea air mixed with Val's distinctive scent. It's an irresistible combination.

Our laughter fades as the wind tousles our hair, and our eyes meet. I freeze—those deep blue eyes, like the sea itself, have held me captive since the moment we met.

Gently, I stroke his cheek, and Val closes his eyes, still smiling that blissful smile. This carefree moment – I try to capture it in my mind like a photograph.

Suddenly, I feel his fingers under my t-shirt, tickling me under my arms and rendering me completely helpless, making me laugh so hard my abs start to hurt.

"Damn, and I'm supposed to be the crazy one?" I gasp, looking up at him again. Val winks at me, and I'm almost tempted to go for his lips when two pairs of shoes walk way too close to our heads, and I immediately feel the curious stares on us.

We get up and brush the sand off our clothes.

"So, what's the plan?" I ask.

"You'll see." His hand slides around my shoulder, resting casually on my neck and pulling me closer. A warm shiver runs through me, and I press closer, the warmth of his skin seeping into mine as I breathe in the mix of salt and the faint scent of his cologne that clings to the hollow of his neck.

"So just the two of us? No audience?" I murmur into his ear.

I hear Val snort softly before he pulls away from me.

"There shouldn't be any audience there."

"Shouldn't?" I ask, suddenly alarmed.

He laughs again. "God, Cas! You'll see soon enough."

We walk a fair distance along the beach, and I start to worry that Val's plan is to hook up in one of those old changing huts scattered along the shore. But I'm wrong. We leave the beach behind and head into town, eventually reaching the harbor. As expected, it's deserted at this hour. All the shops are closed, and only a small harbor pub is still open.

Val stops in front of an old wooden boat. I glance at him, confused. He winks at me before turning his gaze back to the boat. It's got to be at least 40 years old, its extérior coated in black tar paint, with weathered fishing nets hanging off the sides. It doesn't look like it's been out on the water today—or in a while, really. I'm starting to have serious doubts about whatever Val's plan is.

"Come on!" He gestures for me to follow and starts walking up the gangplank. Of course, it has no handrails and creaks and sways ominously with every step Val takes. He finishes with a dramatic jump onto the deck.

He leans over the railing, looking at me expectantly.

"You can't be serious," I say, eyes wide.

"Totally! There's a cabin down there that's pretty cozy—there's even a bed!" He laughs, and I can't tell if it's out of desperation or if he's being serious.

But what choice do I have? Go back to the beach and risk getting caught? No. I finally want to be alone with him—without an audience. This old boat will have to do. Sighing, I step onto the gangplank, which immediately wobbles beneath my feet.

"Who even owns this thing?" I ask, trying to keep my balance, eyeing the dark water below.

"This 'thing' has a name!"

I roll my eyes and take another cautious step toward him. Jeez.

"Christina."

"Great," I mutter, as the plank creaks loudly beneath me.

Val ignores my complaints.

"It belonged to my grandfather," he says. "Now it's my dad's, but it's currently being serviced, so no audience—and no crabs nibbling at you tonight."

Val reaches out his hand, and I quickly grab it, clinging to it as he helps me cross the last bit.

We're still holding hands as I finally reach the boat—'Christina.' Val glances at me, his eyes questioning, and I feel a sudden nervousness rise inside me.

"Everything okay?" he asks.

I shrug, unable to hide my disappointment. "Sorry I couldn't find anything better…"

"Hmm." He smiles, gently brushing my cheek with his left hand. "I think it barely smells like crabs here anymore."

I purse my lips. It definitely smells like diesel and paint, but I keep that thought to myself.

"Come on, I'll show you the rest."

He leads me across the wooden deck to the steering cabin. Inside, there's the wheel and two more doors—one probably leading to a bathroom. The other, which Val opens, leads down into the belly of the ship. He flips on a light that flickers a dull orange above us and heads down first, ducking to avoid hitting his head on the low ceiling.

The smell of wood, salt, and diesel is strong, but I stay quiet. My eyes stay fixed on Val's back, the way his hips sway in front of me—so temptingly.

Does it even matter where we are? As long as we're finally alone together?

I'm surprised when we reach the small sleeping area. It's actually kind of cozy. The bed is freshly made with turquoise bedding, and through the portholes, I can see the sea outside.

"Okay, not as bad as I feared," I smirk.

Val looks pleased. "Yeah?"

I nod, and he watches me from the other side of the bed, a quiet anticipation in his eyes.

Why not? I crawl across the bed toward him, looking up at him from the edge.

A shadow flickers across his face—uncertainty?

Before it can take hold, I pull him down to me, leaving him no choice but to fall forward onto me.

I grab his lips, not letting go. My fingers dance along his side, slipping underneath his t-shirt, feeling the twitch of his muscles as his body tenses briefly again.

I slide my tongue into his mouth, and Val immediately responds, meeting mine with playful intensity, teasing and wrestling as he pants and hums against my lips. His fingers grip my chin, stroking it demandingly, while his other hand moves down to unbutton his jeans. There's no hesitation in his actions, and this sudden dominance, this directness, turns me on more than I expected. There's no cautious exploration between us anymore—just clarity, and yes, we both know exactly what's going to happen tonight.

Val pulls down his jeans along with his tight shorts. His hardness is right there in front of me – for a moment, it startles my mind, but the next moment, I'm practically drooling.

He turns me on so much, and I can't resist a second longer. I close my lips around his cock, circling the tip with my tongue, sucking, licking, and nibbling on it. I taste him, distinct and clear, sweet and earthy. I suck the drops from his slit, whimpering and moaning uncontrollably as I take him deeper into my mouth.

Above me, Val groans loudly, pressing himself closer. God, he's so into this. No matter how much experience he's had with women, right now, he's into me—a guy. And that somehow makes it even better. He wants just me. No other guy, no girl, just me. I take him deeper, forming a ring with my lips and letting him slide far inside, encouraged by the sounds of his loud moans and groans.

I can feel the tension building in his body, the subtle tremors running through his legs, a clear sign that he's right on the edge. His breathing grows heavier, more erratic, and the low groans slipping from his lips grow more desperate. I know he's about to come, and the anticipation sends a rush of heat through me. I brace myself, adjusting slightly as I open my mouth wider, letting his hardness rest against my tongue. I cradle him there, feeling every pulse, every twitch as I take him deeper into my mouth. Val starts thrusting faster, my lips and tongue moving in perfect rhythm with his body.

The salty, earthy taste of him fills my senses, but just as I'm preparing for him to explode, Val suddenly reaches down and grabs my shoulders, pulling me up toward him with a firm yet shaky grip. I'm startled by the sudden movement, but when I meet his eyes, the intensity in his gaze stops me—disbelief, hunger, and something raw.

His chest is heaving, his breath coming in ragged gasps as he stares at me, as if he can't quite believe what's happening, or what's about to.

Without a word, Val's hand slides to the back of my neck, drawing me closer. I can feel the heat radiating off him. His lips crash into mine with a fervor that takes my breath away, his fingers digging into my skin like he's trying to hold onto something solid. The kiss is rough, greedy, and filled with need. There's an urgency beneath it all that catches me off guard—like he's just as consumed by this as I am, unable to resist any longer.

We fall onto the bed together, Val on top of me, devouring my lips. He doesn't seem to care that I taste like him. His kisses are rough, full of hunger, but with every touch, it feels like he's losing control. His left hand slips between us, undoing my pants and sliding under my boxers to grab my cock. A loud whimper escapes me—finally. Val doesn't hesitate, his hand exploring my length with deliberate strokes, rubbing and caressing me in ways that send shivers through my entire body.

I feel him so directly, so close, just as I've wanted all these days.

"More," I gasp.

Val kneels down, tugging at my jeans as I fumble out of my t-shirt. In what feels like ten seconds flat, we're both naked, lying next to each other, just staring. The whole situation feels surreal—being naked together on this slightly swaying boat, just the two of us.

I can feel my cheeks heating up, especially when Val's hand glides down my side, from my shoulders to my hips.

Fuck, I need to tell him. Now's my last chance, I think, dazed, as his hand finds its way to my hardness again.

I pull back slightly, and Val freezes.

"Did I do something wrong?" he asks, concern lacing his voice. I quickly shake my head. "No!" I blurt out, though frustration sneaks into my tone.

"It's just… I should probably tell you that I… uh…" I trail off, struggling to get the words out. It's embarrassing and feels kind of dumb.

Val gently strokes my cheek. "You okay?"

"Yeah."

"Cas?"

I take a deep breath. "It's… my first time… doing this."

There, I've said it. My face burns even hotter.

Val blinks at me, looking thoughtful. Then he starts to grin, leaning in to plant a kiss on my cheek.

"I wouldn't have guessed that," he whispers in my ear.

I pull my head back a bit, looking at him questioningly.

"Well…" He laughs. "I got the impression you wanted to devour me whole at our first date."

"Well, yeah," I mutter awkwardly. It feels like that was ages ago now.

"That's not really me, though." It probably sounds unbelievable to him, but just thinking about how I used to be with Finn reminds me of how reserved and closed off I was. It's a miracle we even lasted three months.

"No?"

"No." I grab his hand, seeking reassurance, feeling the warmth of his skin.

"You're not like that either, right?" I add hesitantly.

He shakes his head. "Not for a long time," he says quietly.

He kisses me again, this time on the forehead. "And this, just us, is more than enough, okay? It doesn't have to be anything more."

I nod, feeling a wave of relief wash over me—it takes the pressure off. As much as I like Val, as much as I want him, my own unpredictable reactions scare me. And I don't know anyone whose first time didn't come with pain. Even Finn had described his first experience with dread.

Val doesn't have much experience in this area either, and with him, it would definitely be painful. That fear is growing bigger now that I'm so close to what I've been yearning for.

"It's already amazing just the way it is," he grins at me.

"Really?"

"Oh God, Cas, you're incredible—like a hurricane that's completely turned my world upside down."

"And that's a good thing?" I ask, unsure.

He grabs my lips again. "Fuck, yes," he murmurs into the kiss. "A really good thing!"

I grin, pushing him back a little to study him—his flushed cheeks, swollen lips, and those icy blue eyes.

Then, his expression shifts, growing more serious. "Honestly, Cas, you're the best thing that's happened to me in... forever." His hand tightens around mine. "Whatever happens tonight, I won't forget this—or you." His voice wavers slightly, and when he smiles, my stomach does flips.

He really likes me. Likes me for who I am, as crazy as that sounds.

With a contented sigh, I press myself against him again, wrapping him in my arms, holding him so tight that Val ends up flat on his back, with me lying fully on top of him. I grin into his neck, feeling nothing but pure happiness. It just feels so right.

"I kind of like you too," I giggle into his ear.

As if those words were even necessary after everything I've done over the past few days to show him just how much I'm into him.

I feel his chest rise and fall as he chuckles softly.

"Good," he replies.

Chapter 12

Val's lips press into mine, deepening the kiss as his hands glide lower, each stroke leaving a trail of fire along my spine until his fingers hover at the edge of my waistband. My breath catches, the warmth of his touch sinking through me.

"Is this okay?" he murmurs in my ear.

I nod, staying on top of him, savoring every second. His fingers glide down my spine, tracing the curve of my ass, brushing lightly against my thighs. They run along the cleft, barely grazing the soft fuzz, but it feels so damn good.

A soft whimper escapes me. His heartbeat pounds beneath me, but I can't even find the energy to kiss him back. His fingers alone feel so incredible right there, in that one perfect spot.

Val's touch is deliberate, every stroke of his fingers feather-light, as if I'm something rare, delicate. The way he moves—slow, reverent—sends shivers across my skin, unraveling any tension left within me.

"Val," I gasp as his fingers glide over the middle of my butt.

"More!"

I hear his quiet laugh underneath me.

"You sure?"

"Totally sure," I whimper back.

He gently shifts from beneath me, his gaze catching mine with an unspoken question. The flicker of uncertainty in his eyes, the way his fingers linger on my hip, waiting for my response—it's all an electric charge humming between us.

I just nod, and Val pulls a small bottle of lube out from under the pillow.

"I'm not going to do anything you don't want," he says seriously. I sit beside him, eyeing the plain little tube as my hand brushes against his.

"I know," I say, then grab his lips, nibbling and sucking on them.

Val presses me back down onto the bed, and I take a shaky breath, willing myself to relax as his fingers slide over my back, massaging my shoulders and neck, occasionally slipping lower, brushing over my butt. Each pass is a teasing promise—barely there, yet enough to send my mind spiraling between craving more and holding back. My skin prickles under his touch, heat pooling low in my stomach, as anticipation and nerves twist together.

I want more, but at the same time, it already feels so unbelievably good just being touched by him this gently. I can lie in front of him completely at ease, fully trusting that he won't push things any further without my say-so.

His lips trace down my neck, nibbling softly, his body pressing close against mine before he pulls back a little and continues massaging my shoulders and neck.

I have no idea how much time passes—seconds, minutes, maybe even hours—it feels timeless with him, like the rules outside this room no longer apply.

His lips trail down my spine, kissing every ridge and hollow along the way. I feel goosebumps rising on my skin, drawing a soft, pleased hum from Val. When he reaches my tailbone and runs his tongue over that spot, I can't hold back a needy whimper.

"More?" Val's deep voice rumbles as his hands grip my butt cheeks, pulling them apart, making me swallow hard. Before I can answer or let any doubts surface, my ass lifts instinctively, practically begging him to take me.

Val hisses behind me.

"Fuck, Cas, you look so hot."

Hot—that's the perfect word for this. My crazy state, my lack of restraint. He's seen every inch of me now, knows all the wild thoughts I have about him. I can feel the pulsing running through my cock, vibrating through my whole body.

Val is everything I want. I whimper, looking back at him longingly.

This boy, who's staring directly and intensely at my ass with those icy blue eyes, biting hard on his lower lip.

"So damn sexy," he gasps, still not looking at me—instead, Val is suddenly everywhere. His tongue is right there, without warning, at my most intimate spot, sending me reeling within a second.

I can't control my body anymore, I can only arch into him, completely unrestrained and utterly willing. Val manages to slide the tip of his tongue inside me, making me gasp and moan loudly.

A storm of curses and groans escapes me.

How can something feel *this* insanely good?

No one has ever done this before, so directly, so passionately.

He licks eagerly over my entrance, kneading my ass, burying his face between my cheeks, whimpering lustfully into me. His tongue pushes back inside me, and my entire body shudders. I bury my head in the pillow, gripping the sheets and the edge of the bed.

"Val!" I moan far too loudly. "Fuck! So damm good!"

His fingers glide over my hole, pressing inside me, but there's no pain. The second finger follows, stretching me, sliding in and out, and I breathe harder and faster.

Val flips me over—I'm dizzy, letting him take charge—lying on my back, looking at him, giving him all the confirmation he needs. He spreads my legs, his fingers plunging inside me again, each thrust deliberate and holding my gaze like a magnetic attraction. His eyes—glowing with pure hunger—mirror the same need that's consuming me, a feverish desire coursing through every nerve in my body. He can see how much I want him, how much I crave this—*him*, inside me.

I gasp and pant with each thrust, his fingers plunging deeper. A third finger slips in, and the pace quickens.. *God*. Val's fucking me with his fingers while his other hand pumps his own hard cock.

His usually cool blue eyes turn darker, hungrier.

Fuck, he's into this, I realize. And maybe I'm the first person he's ever explored this fantasy with.

"Cas," he growls, glancing back at the heated connection between us. His fingers buried deep inside me while he strokes himself harder and faster. Pre-cum starts to leak out, slicking his tip and fingers.

"Do it!" I rasp. I want—no, I need—to have his hard cock right between my legs, to finally experience what it feels like.

Val groans, plunging his fingers into me once more and hitting that divine spot inside me unexpectedly. I scream out, throwing my head back, moaning, cursing, gasping.

"Please, fuck me!" I plead.

Val doesn't say a word—he's on me in an instant, spreading my legs wider, and instinctively I hook one leg over his shoulder, wanting him deep, all the way in.

No more preparation. Val, his tip right at my entrance, pushing inside me, unstoppable, sliding deeper and deeper. Immediately, I feel the unfamiliar stretch, the burning within. I press my lips together. It's intense—the pain crashes through me, gripping me all over. Harsh and relentless.

"Val!" I whimper. Too much—too much of him, all at once. Tears sting my eyes, and my body tightens.

Val pulls out instantly, staring at me in shock, sitting up and putting some distance between us.

No! I think, panicking. Don't stop!

I grab his shoulder, pulling him back down toward me. His body feels tense, rigid.

A troubled shadow crosses his face.

"Shit, I lost control!" he grits out angrily.

I shake my head quickly. "I'm fine!"

"No!" he snaps, his voice laced with frustration. His eyes flash with regret.

I don't want him to stop now, for this incredible night to be over already.

Yeah, it stung for a moment, but he didn't cause any more pain and stopped immediately when he noticed.

"I'm fine!" I assure him.

He looks at me doubtfully.

"Really." I grin knowingly.

He closes his eyes for a moment, weighing my words. I take advantage of that, sliding my hands around his neck, pulling him back down on top of me, positioning his still rock-hard cock right at my entrance. I grind against it, and I feel Val's mind shut off again.

"I don't want to hurt you," he whimpers, one last attempt as he tries to pull away again.

"You're not!" My lips latch onto his, clinging to them, and then I'm the one guiding his entry.

Val stays still, a muscle twitching in his jaw as I take control. Let his tip glide teasingly against my hole over and over again—his breathing stutters and I feel the tension tightening in his body, fighting the urge to just give in.

It feels so damn good, just like his tongue earlier. Val gasps, his body trembling with restraint. I know how much effort it's taking him to hold back, to not just thrust forward and drive into me. A thin layer of sweat forms on his forehead, and his hot breath brushes against my cheek and nose.

A forbidden thought crosses my mind, and I dare to act on it, sliding my hand down to the base of his spine, trailing my fingers delicately down between his butt cheeks.

Val instantly melts, letting out an unexpected moan as I inch closer to that tempting spot.

He sinks down onto me even further. I keep going, tracing between his ass cheeks until I dare to run a finger right over his hole. His reaction is immediate—a breathy moan escapes him as he presses back against my fingers. Surprised, I pause for a moment, unable to hide a grin. But he doesn't notice, his face buried against my neck, panting heavily against my skin.

I glide back between his cheeks, and again he gasps.

Fuck, he's really into this.

Val's head, his nose, his lips slide along my neck, down to my collarbone, my chest, where he rests, breathing heavily, leaving me free to explore.

I glance at him in surprise—his eyes are closed, fully focused on my touch.

I pull my fingers back briefly, wetting them in my mouth before returning, this time directly to his most intimate spot. His body jerks like he's been electrocuted. I latch onto his gaping mouth, pressing my lips against his, while my fingers and tongue slide into both of his openings simultaneously. A deep growl rumbles from him.

Val arches his back, pressing into my touch, looking completely lost in the moment as I delve deeper into him, feeling the warmth and tightness around my fingers.

This can't be the first time he's been touched like this, I think. Maybe it wasn't another person—maybe it was just him. Curiosity surges through me, and I'm about to ask him so many things, but a single heated moan from Val right next to my ear pulls my own mind back into this intense pleasure between us.

My cock is rock hard, getting even more stimulation from Val's movements as it keeps sliding against his flat stomach, rubbing against him. Drops of precum spill out of me uncontrollably, and I can't think straight anymore—I just want him.

With my left hand, I reach between us, needing to feel him so badly. I grab his cock and guide it to my entrance. The next time I add a third finger and let it slide in, the same thing happens to me—his cock slowly but steadily pushes inside me, and this time, there's no pain, just a slight burn mixed with an indescribable pleasure.

Val, above me, lets out a loud, almost primal groan, completely uninhibited. Completely himself.

"Cas, fuck!" he hisses, pausing as he fills me completely, all the way to the hilt. I close my eyes, breathing heavily. Incredible—it's the only word that fits, along with the sensation of Val's huge cock stretching me.

Him, all of this. My arms wrap tightly around his back, pulling him as close as possible, feeling like we're one. My soulmate, my missing link, my better half. He's here, with me, as close as anyone could ever be.

I feel Val's breath syncing with mine, his heartbeat matching the rhythm of my own. Even the heavy, husky moans escaping his mouth sound just like mine.

A realization settles deep in my chest, an ache that is both beautiful and terrifying—this connection, this moment, this is something I will never find again. Val—my first and possibly only love. My fingers tighten around his back, as if if I let go, I would lose everything I didn't even know I needed until now. Val has become more than a fleeting crush; he has imprinted himself in places I didn't even know could feel so much.

"Casper," Val breathes, his voice shaking with something raw and tender as he begins to move inside me. My grip loosens, my free hand sliding down his back as I look into those ice-blue eyes—no longer cold, but warm and open. They glow with more than just lust—something deeper, as if he's finally breaking down the walls and letting me see the affection and joy he's kept hidden.

Chapter 13

Like a knot, tightly intertwined, connected through every possible point—this is the best way to describe having sex with Val. He's lying behind me, arms wrapped securely around my chest, one hand gripping my cock while my fingers are buried as deep as they can go between his cheeks. My range of motion is minimal, he's pressing against me so tightly, so intensely, wanting everything. His sweaty cheek rubs against mine, his moans echoing like a volcano right into my ear.

The friction between us, this connection, his lips desperately seeking mine—*God*, and his cock, buried deep inside me. Val holds still, moving only slightly, but he's right where I can feel him most. His tip presses against my prostate, making me see stars, completely sending me off. My muscles twitch, adjusting, my body trembling with longing anticipation. But I don't want to come yet—I want to savor this feeling of him as long as I can. So intertwined, so connected, so together.

There's this wild fluttering in my stomach—Val's completely taken me over, completely captured me. Like a lightning strike, I freeze, taking in his scent as he steadily but slowly pumps into me, pressing his lips against my neck, kissing and sucking on me.

"Casper," he murmurs hoarsely, and a wide grin spreads across my face. My fingers delve deeper into him, drawing a helpless moan from him.

"Fuck, I'm gonna come soon," he barely manages to rasp out.

"Then come," I whisper back. "Come inside me!"

A low growl escapes him. "Shit, I want to feel you when I do!"

I pause, looking back at him in surprise.

"In me," he groans, pure lust dripping from his voice—words he'd probably never say when sober.

Everything inside me tightens at the thought of feeling Val that way—it's too much, too tempting. I push back hard against him, feeling him deep inside me, and I whimper as I come hard, pulsing. My cum shoots out in all directions, but it's not the end, just the beginning.

Behind me, I hear Val groan my name darkly, feel the heat spreading inside me as his cock swells even more.

I want more, is all I can think. I glance back at him, see the wide grin on his face, knowing he's still floating somewhere far from here, just like me. He doesn't resist when I pounce on him, kissing him like there's no tomorrow, like this is our first and last night. And he doesn't resist when I spread his legs and slide my still rock-hard cock between his cheeks.

"I need you," I whimper. "This." And with those words, I push into him. Val's eyes widen before he fully grasps what's happening, but his body doesn't resist. Val takes a deep breath and then visibly relaxes.

No, he doesn't tense up, not at all. I push deeper and deeper into him, feeling the incredible heat and tightness around my cock. If I hadn't just come, I'd do it now—it feels that good, so raw, so perfect.

Val wraps his long legs around me, pressing closer. I don't even have a choice—I can only thrust into him, as deep as possible.

I latch onto his neck with my lips, letting my body take control. I don't know what I'm doing, but instinct takes over, guiding my hips to lift and thrust in a quick rhythm, driving deep into this incredible boy. I hear and feel his wild heartbeat beneath me, feel his cock hardening again, pressing against my stomach. I feel his fingers digging into my back, into my hair.

"Fuck, so good!" he moans deeply.

I'm soaring, flying too close to the sun, completely intoxicated by Val. There's no turning back from here. I lose myself in him, taking him harder, deeper, more recklessly, more freely. Val responds to every thrust with a moan of pleasure, urging me on, pushing me past my limits and beyond.

It's Val who finally flips us over, looking at me knowingly before straddling me again, sliding my cock deep into himself in one swift motion, taking what he needs so badly.

Val, riding me up and down, completely lost in the moment, using my cock to hit that perfect spot inside him and sending me spiraling into bliss again.

The sight of him on top of me—those focused, cool blue eyes, that dreamy yet lustful look he gives me. He leans back, taking me as deep as possible.

Our sounds fill the air—ragged moans and gasps echo around us. I feel Val so tight against me, my tip hitting that perfect spot inside him over and over. He throws his head back, mouth wide open—one last thrust, and I don't even have to touch him—Val comes hard, collapsing on top of me. I feel it all, his cum spurting out, covering my chin, chest, and stomach. But instead of pulling away, I push into that pleasure. Val's tight ring milks my cock, and I come, deep inside him. Different from before, but just as good.

Sweaty and blissed out, we lie there entangled, still wrapped up in each other. Val's head rests against my chest, his breath still coming fast and heavy.

It takes time for us to come back down, for each of us to settle back into our bodies.

"Incredible," I rasp out.

It's the only word that comes to mind. How can sex feel this good? How is it possible for our bodies to connect so intensely, so powerfully?

Val slides down beside me, curling up close behind me. I hear his soft laugh, but I don't have the energy to look up. Exhaustion fills every corner of my body, my eyes closing for a moment, drifting off until Val's deep voice pulls me back.

"I'm sorry I was such an asshole to you at first."

I let out a tired hum. He's more than made up for that tonight.

"It's okay," I murmur, instinctively snuggling closer to him, eyes still closed, feeling his arms wrap around me like a cocoon.

Everything between us is sticky, and I feel the lingering tremors of our connection all over my body. My muscles twitch from the strain, my ass aches and burns a bit, but I don't care. If I had even a shred of energy left, I'd do it all over again right now. Honestly, I can't get enough of this blue-haired boy, never.

"You're way too good for me," he whispers, barely audible. His eyes flicker down, like he can't stand to meet mine. I stare at him, stunned, my chest tight with something close to anger.

"That's bullshit."

He lets out a long, shaky breath, his shoulders sagging. "You don't get it, Cas. Right now, here, with us, it's perfect… but after this, it's all downhill. It always is."

I pull away from his arms, turning to face him with a warning look.

"Stop talking like that."

He closes his eyes for a moment.

"That's how it always goes. In the end, I mess it up, every damn time."

I snort.

"I honestly don't see how you could screw this up—how you could break this—" I gesture at us and the messy bed.

He looks at me with a pained expression, sitting up and rubbing his face. Finally, he meets my gaze again, and the coldness is back in his eyes.

"I'm not like this," he says quietly.

I glare at him.

"I can't do it—a relationship with you, or with anyone else. I mess it up every time."

An exasperated sigh escapes me.

"Why are you talking such bullshit? This just started between us, why are you already trying to end it?"

"I don't want that," he grumbles. "But it's inevitably where it's headed."

"Yeah, just like one day we'll all drop dead and die!" I snap.

A shadow crosses his face. Val looks like everything inside him tightens painfully for a moment.

"You don't get it, and damn it, Cas, you barely know me." His fingers gently brush through my hair as he speaks. "I've messed up so much, hurt so many people... Even when I tried, I ended up ruining everything." I watch as Val swallows hard, his fingers trembling slightly as he brushes a sweaty strand from my forehead.

I shake my head, refusing to believe him. "You're way too hard on yourself—so many people care about you." My mind drifts back to the beach concert, where he laughed and talked with all those people. They weren't strangers—they were his friends.

"God, Val and you know how much I care about you. It doesn't matter how long I've known you or how well— you felt it too, you had to feel it!" I glance at him, hesitantly. "Didn't you?"

He nods, barely, and I exhale in relief.

"Then why are you talking about giving up? Because you're scared?"

"I'm not scared... I'm just saying you'd be better off forgetting about tonight, about me."

I glare at him, furious.

"Why are you trying so hard to push me away?"

Val suddenly stands up, pausing for a moment as he stares at the ship's wall. I see his muscles tense, watch him hold himself back.

"I didn't leave Berlin by choice," he finally says, still not looking at me, still not coming back to bed.

I really messed up there," he says, each word weighed down with regret. I sit on the edge of the bed, trying to reach for him, but he jerks his hand back like my touch might burn him. The silence stretches out, heavy and suffocating. "You can tell me… but you don't have to." My voice is low, careful, like I'm stepping over broken glass.

"No," he says louder, turning to face me with a look that chills me to the bone. Val looks shattered—his usual confident exterior crumbling as he struggles to speak. His hands are trembling as he wipes them over his face, like he's trying to scrub away something he can't escape. His voice is raw when he finally speaks.

"Cas, I'm on probation." The words hang between us like a threat, and my stomach tightens with dread. "What? Why?" I ask, my voice barely holding steady as I search his eyes for answers.

With a deep sigh, he sits back down beside me, careful to keep his body from touching mine.

"It was an accident…" he whispers.

"What happened?" Panic grips me. My heart insists it's impossible, but my mind warns me that something was always off with him.

I… I killed my girlfriend." The confession comes out broken, like it's been tearing him apart inside for months. He shoots to his feet, pacing like he's trying to outrun his own guilt. His eyes are glassy, the tears barely held back, and his throat bobs as he swallows, again and again, like he's choking on the words. "Damn it, Cas, I let her die!" The last word shatters, and his breath catches, ragged and uneven.

I back away even more. No, that can't be! You don't get only probation for murder.

"We were both completely messed up, drunk, high on all kinds of drugs. Fuck… and Zoe drove that night." His voice becomes shrill and panicked, as if he can still see the moment playing out in front of him.

"I didn't stop her, I let her drive, I let her die." He stops, pressing his trembling lips together. They're shaking, just like the rest of his body.

"We slammed right into a tree," he says quietly. "We were both thrown from the car on impact, and for some reason, I survived while Zoe died almost instantly." Val buries his face in his hands, and I sit there, frozen, staring at him in shock.

Short and brutal—the end of a relationship, of a whole life. Val has blood on his hands.

"Fuck, Cas," he sobs. "I don't deserve to be out here, living this pathetic life." His voice cracks. "Even totally wasted, I knew it was a terrible idea to let Zoe drive—" His words cut off, his eyes overflowing as I sit beside him, still frozen, feeling utterly numb.

Suddenly, so much makes sense—his distant behavior, his constant worry about me, the alcohol, the weed, and why he no longer has a driver's license.

"But you didn't kill her," I finally whisper after what feels like an eternity.

He looks at me bitterly, wiping away the tears.

"I wasn't convicted for it, just for the drugs I had on me. But yeah, without me, she never would've driven that night, and she never would've started using. Shit, she was from here! This was her home! Berlin, that city—it wasn't where she was meant to be, it wasn't her place." He pauses, staring out the porthole at the waves. "She only moved there for me, for my career. Damn it, she was always by my side, always supporting me... And then, just like that, it was all over. Zoe was gone, didn't exist anymore, and fuck," he chokes out. "Believe me, I tried more than once to end this torture, I didn't want to live anymore."

Tears stream down my face, and I can't stop them, can't hold them back.

My body moves before my mind. Without thinking, I wrap my arms around him, holding his trembling frame tightly. "I'm so glad you're here, that you're alive," I whisper into his ear, pressing a gentle kiss against his skin.

His eyes lock onto mine, wide and searching, like he's looking for some sign that I'll leave him too.

"Why?" His voice trembles, barely hanging on.

"Why what?" I ask, my own voice softer now, steady but searching.

"Why are you still here with me?" I can't help the small smile tugging at my lips. "I don't know... I just couldn't walk away. It's been like that from the start."

Val sighs, his chest rising and falling as if he's letting go of a weight Shaking his head, he wipes away the last of his tears, a dry, bitter laugh escaping. "That didn't exactly do you any favors, did it?" His laugh is strained, tinged with something between irony and defeat—like a final aftershock of a long-past earthquake.

His girlfriend is gone—a tragedy that still haunts him. But deep down, I know it wasn't his fault. We all make choices, take roads we never expected. Zoe made hers that night, just like I've made mine. And Val? He's carrying a burden that was never his to bear.

He forces a smile, but it's fragile, cracked at the edges. "You're a damn hurricane, you know that? And no matter what, not even all this shit can drive you away from me."

"It won't," I say, my voice thick with determination. "Nothing and no one can."

Chapter 14

over a year later

Not exactly how I imagined waking up on my 18th birthday: head pounding, body aching, and not even in my own bed. My skin itches against unfamiliar sheets, and the headache feels like someone's drilling into my skull. Everything feels wrong—the air, the light, even the bed beneath me. The last thing I wanted was to start this day with a hangover, in someone else's bed, feeling lost in the mess I've made for myself.

I can't even open my eyes; they sting, stuck together. I feel around—satin sheets and warm skin—a body lying still beside me. A frustrated groan escapes me. Not good, not at all. I take a deep breath, trying to get a grip on the dizziness and nausea swirling inside me. Memories from last night slip through my mind like sand through fingers—fleeting, blurry, impossible to hold on to.

Finally, I manage to sit up and pry my eyes open. There's a mop of curly brown hair half-buried under the blanket. Justin? Or maybe Finn? Hard to tell. The night is a foggy blur that refuses to clear—just flashes of loud music, flashing lights, and too many drinks.

Yeah, we celebrated—hard. Celebrated into my birthday, and I let myself be the center of it—too much, too wild, and there go all my promises and resolutions, broken again.

The haze in my head starts to lift, and the night begins to come back into focus. Before all of this started, Finn had cooked for me at his apartment, and we watched a movie. It was fine. Something we've done so many times before—so predictable, so safe. But damn, it was my 18th birthday—I didn't want to sit on the couch like an old married couple with Finn and watch TV. But Finn is just Finn. He doesn't drink, hardly goes out anymore, and definitely not to the same clubs as me. I wanted something more exciting, something wild.

I shrug, thinking back to the moment it all started. Samuel, I remember now, and a cold shiver runs through me. He was the one who texted, asking if I wanted to celebrate properly, saying he'd "take care of everything." Shit, and he did—slipping cash to the bouncer to get us in, making sure we had a VIP spot, even buying round after round of drinks. He made it clear what he wanted in return, though. Samuel's been hitting on me for weeks—mid-forties, trying way too hard to appear younger, but there's something about him that scares even me. He's not the type I'd usually go for, but he's persistent, and last night, I was too far gone to push him away.

The memory sends another chill down my spine. Close call—for me, at least. Samuel definitely hoped I'd wake up in his bed this morning, not Justin's. There was a point in the night where I almost gave in—his hand on my back, his breath too close, whispering things I didn't want to hear but couldn't fully block out. I was teetering on the edge, ready to fall into whatever trap he was laying. But then Justin showed up after his shift, just in time to pull me out. I was already pretty drunk when he saw me with Samuel, and from what little I remember, he must've seen the warning signs and stepped in.

Justin's the bartender at the Cave, always has been—a wildcard with a good heart. He's only two years older than me, but somehow he still holds onto that wild energy, always ready for the next crazy adventure.

Last night, he saved me from making a huge mistake, and for that, I'm grateful. But waking up in his bed doesn't feel much better.

Justin is a good friend, nothing more, and whatever happened between us shouldn't have been part of my birthday celebration.

I remember him grabbing my hand, pulling me onto the dance floor, and we started dancing—our bodies swaying in the dark, our hands brushing against each other, the smell of sweat and cologne thick in the air.

With that mischievous glint in his eyes, I couldn't say no to him. And damn, I really did have fun with him, at least for a while. We laughed, we joked, and somewhere in the blur, after I popped a pill to keep the buzz going, his arm slipped around my waist. At first, it was subtle, just friendly, but the more we drank and the more the stimulant kicked in, the closer we got until it wasn't just friendly anymore.

When the bar started clearing out, Justin leaned in, his lips brushing against my ear as he whispered, "Let's get out of here."

I was drunk—too drunk to think straight, too drunk to remember all the promises I made to myself about taking it easy, about staying in control. And it wasn't just the alcohol; the pill I'd taken earlier was coursing through my system, making everything feel distant and hazy.

In that moment, with the stimulant numbing my senses and Justin's hand on my back, guiding me out of the club, I didn't care.

We stumbled back to his apartment, laughing at stupid jokes, our voices echoing off the empty streets. Once we got inside, it was like a switch flipped. The laughter died down, replaced by the tension that had been building all night. He pushed me against the wall as soon as the door closed, his lips crashing into mine, hot and demanding. It was messy—hands grabbing, clothes tugged off in a frenzy. We didn't make it far; we barely made it to his bed before we were all over each other.

Justin was relentless, and so was I. The alcohol dulled the edges of everything, made us bolder, rougher. It was a blur of sweaty skin, tangled sheets, and rough, heated kisses. I remember the sound of his voice in my ear, low and throaty, telling me how good I felt, how much he wanted this. And I let him take the lead, let him show me what he wanted—what I wanted too, even though I knew I'd regret it the next morning.

I can't pinpoint when it got out of hand—when it went from fun to frantic. I remember feeling trapped in that pink satin, the sheets sticking to our damp skin as he moved above me. He was rougher than I expected, his fingers, slick with lube, sliding between my cheeks, then pressing into me. His breath was hot on my neck as he whispered, "Just relax." The pain of his cock entering me is still vivid in my mind—pain mixed with pleasure in a way that left me gasping for air. I let him do it, let him take what he wanted, because in that moment, I didn't care about anything else. I wanted to forget everything, to lose myself in someone else, and Justin gave me that escape.

When it was over, we lay there in the dark, tangled together, both of us too spent to move. Justin was still panting, his chest heaving against mine as he muttered something about how wild it had been, how he hadn't had a night like that in ages. I didn't respond—I just stared at the ceiling, trying to push away the creeping guilt that was starting to settle in. I knew I'd hate myself for it in the morning, but it was too late by then. I'd already made my bed, and now I was lying in it—literally.

I sit up and take a deep breath, trying to push the memories away. Justin is still half-asleep, curled up under the pink satin sheets, looking younger and more innocent than either of us really are. I quickly get dressed, avoiding looking at him, I grab my clothes from the floor.

"Just," I mumble, finally getting to my feet.

"Mm," comes a sleepy murmur from the bed.

"I'm heading out."

"Mm."

"Alright," I say with a sigh. Justin will probably spend half the day in bed. He is the ultimate night owl, something I was myself a few months ago and have always admired about him. Nobody is full of energy and crazy ideas at 3 a.m. like this guy with the curls. But during the day? Forget it.

"Coffee?" comes a quiet, dazed offer.

"No, I'm fine. I have to go anyway."

"OK." There's a rustling under the blanket. Justin looks up at me, sleepy and blinking. His eyes squint as he gives me a quick glance, probably harsh without his glasses or contacts.

"Are you okay?" He groans and rubs his face. "Shit, last night was intense." He yawns loudly.

"Yes," I answer shortly. "But I really have to go now."

He nods and sits up, the sheet slipping down over his slender torso, exposing the base of his flaccid penis. Of course, he's naked. Before I can stop myself, a frustrated groan escapes my lips. This is a disaster, and I have no one to blame but myself.

What we did last night is written all over this bed, in this room, even in the air. It's stuffy, smells of sweat, too much testosterone and sex. To complete the picture, tissues and open condom wrappers are scattered on the floor.

I pause for a moment. It's not just my head that hurts, but my ass too. Another flash—Justin's hands gripping my hips, that urgent, "I need you so bad." Everything was raw, chaotic, and completely reckless. But now, it's too late to think about it.

"Hey, text me, okay?" Justin mumbles, rolling back into bed, clutching the pink blanket between his knees, curling up like a kid.

I nod. "Yeah... we'll see."

With that, I slip on my t-shirt and leave the tiny apartment at the train station as fast as I can.

*

It's already past noon when I finally stumble back home. The sun's harsh light doesn't do my pounding head any favors, and I already know this will probably be one of the worst birthdays ever. Damn it, and it's my eighteenth. But I messed up again. I guess I deserve it.

My hand shakes as I fumble with the front door key. Inside, the silence hits me like a wall, and the weak "Hey" I mutter to the empty space feels lost. I step into the kitchen, the usual comforting smell of home doing nothing to calm the knot in my stomach. On the dining table sits a small chocolate cake with a single candle stuck in the middle, flickering like a sad, quiet reminder of something I'd rather not face today.

I freeze, breath catching in my throat. Music drifts faintly from upstairs, probably from my sisters' rooms, but down here… it's just me. A folded note rests beside the cake, the handwriting familiar and full of love. "Happy Birthday, Casper. May all your dreams come true. Love, Mom and Dad."

A frustrated growl slips out, surprising even me. My dreams—what the hell are those anymore?

Last year, I could've answered that question without even thinking. Val. Back then, he was still a huge part of my life. He'd video-call me, and we'd talk for over an hour. He even sent me a necklace—a small glass capsule filled with sand from our beach. God, just thinking about it makes me groan, rough and bitter.

The last thing I want is to dwell on him, but I can't help it. My fingers itch, so I check my phone, scrolling through the birthday messages—dozens of well-meaning wishes from friends and acquaintances, but nothing from him. Maybe he'll text later, maybe tonight. But that small, hollow hope doesn't do much to fill the emptiness I'm feeling right now.

Sighing, I grab a plate from the cupboard and slice into the cake. The knife glides through the chocolate frosting and vanilla cream with ease, but after a few bites, it all turns to ash in my mouth. My stomach lurches, and I barely make it to the guest bathroom before I'm throwing up the night and the last shred of my dignity.

Panting, I flush the toilet and slump against the cool tiles. The hard surface digs into my back, grounding me in the reality of what I've become. I stare into the full-length mirror opposite, barely recognizing the person staring back. I've changed—outwardly, sure. My hair's longer now, almost chin-length, and my face has lost the softness of youth, replaced with sharper angles that don't feel like mine. I've grown taller, stronger, but none of it feels right. My brown eyes look dead—tired and dull, with dark circles underneath that tell the real story. My lips are cracked and swollen, and faint, ghostly fingerprints mar the skin of my neck, reminders of last night's reckless abandon.

How did I lose control again? I promised myself things would be different now—that I wouldn't drink so much and get high again, that I wouldn't let myself get dragged into the darkness again. And yet, here I am, stuck in an endless loop, making the same mistakes over and over, like a broken record that can't help but replay the same miserable song.

It all started with Charlie, the first to show me how easy it is to lose control, how tempting it is to do the things you shouldn't.

It feels like I'm fighting a losing battle. I can't find balance—I'm always teetering on the edge, pushing too far, breaking boundaries, tripping over the same mistakes until I'm back on the ground. I'm not a rebel—that's not what drives me to mess up so much. Maybe it's an addiction to that brief feeling of being above everything—above the law when I break a window, the thrill of sneaking into gay clubs through the back door, the rush of flirting with men twice my age, the recklessness of taking drugs I barely know anything about.

A dry laugh escapes me, the sound twisted and hollow. At least I'm alone right now, not having to face my parents' looks of disappointment. One look from them, and they'd know instantly. Sure, I could try to talk my way out of it, claim I stayed at Finn's, but I suspect he's already been here and ruined that option.

I'm too much—for him, for my parents, for my close friends. They can't stand me anymore—how could they, when I can barely stand myself? For the guys at the clubs, I'm just a thrilling, pretty toy to play with. But they'd never want more than that, never go deeper. They might scratch the surface at most, but even if they did, they'd only find shards.

God, I'm so tired. So fucking tired of everything. I lean back and bang my head against the tiles, the dull thud barely registering through the fog in my mind. All I want is to crawl into bed and forget it all, to sink into oblivion and never come up for air again.

A ringing sound shatters the silence, pulling me from my dark thoughts and making me flinch. Struggling to my feet, I quickly wash my face with cold water, trying to rinse away the guilt and shame clinging to my skin. I hope it's just the mail, a package to distract me from the mess I've made.

But to my dismay, it's Finn standing at the door, his face a mask of concern and frustration. He doesn't say anything at first, just looks at me, taking a deep breath like he's steeling himself for what's coming next.

"Wow," he finally sighs, the disappointment in his voice cutting through me like a knife.

"I'm gonna take a shower," I mumble, desperate for an escape.

He snorts, stepping inside and closing the door behind him.

"Don't bother."

I roll my eyes, heading to the kitchen and dropping onto a chair at the dining table, my body heavy with exhaustion.

"You want something?" I push the cake in his direction, through the thought of eating it again makes my stomach churn.

Finn eyes the cake thoughtfully, his expression unreadable. After a moment, he shakes his head and moves to the fancy coffee machine, starting to brew two cups of black coffee. He's quiet as he works, the silence between us thick and uncomfortable. When the coffee's ready, he sets a cup in front of me, along with a small package, neatly wrapped in blue paper.

"Happy Birthday," he mutters, the words heavy with unspoken concern.

Guilt twists inside me, sharp and unrelenting, stabbing at my already fragile composure. I open my mouth to speak, to explain, but the words get tangled up in my throat.

"I didn't want... I meant to—" I start to stammer, but Finn cuts me off.

"Don't. I'm tired of hearing your excuses."

I sigh, the weight of his words pressing down on me.

"So am I," I admit quietly, my voice barely above a whisper.

Finn looks at me sadly, his light brown eyes filled with a worry that I don't deserve. He drops into the chair next to mine, his presence a reminder of everything I've been trying to avoid.

"Why didn't you just stay with me last night?" His voice is gentle, but there's an edge of frustration to it, like he's trying to understand something he can't quite grasp.

I shrug, wanting to lie, but one look into Finn's worried eyes forces the truth out of me.

"Got an invite to the Cave." A cold shiver runs down my spine as I think about Samuel again. Maybe I should text Justin after all; in my totally messed-up state last night, he had saved me from that creep.

"And you couldn't say no to that, of course," Finn's voice is distant, muffled by the layers of my own guilt.

I take a deep breath, trying to gather the courage to face him.

"I wanted to cancel," I mutter half-heartedly, knowing it's a lie even as I say it.

Finn crosses his arms over his chest, his posture tense.

"Were you in that club all night?" He looks at me seriously, his eyes searching mine for answers I'm not sure I have.

"Does it even matter now?" I reply, avoiding his gaze.

Finn runs a hand through his dark blonde hair, sighing deeply, the sound heavy with disappointment.

"Everyone's worried," he says, his voice softening.

"I know," I whisper.

Hesitantly, I pick up Finn's gift, examining it with a mixture of curiosity and guilt.

"What's in here?" I ask, trying to lighten the mood, but my voice comes out flat, devoid of any real enthusiasm.

"Just open it," he says, his tone gentle but firm.

I tear open the wrapping quickly, revealing a simple bracelet with a black stone attached to it.

"An opal," Finn explains quietly. "It's supposed to protect you."

The gesture is so sweet, so unexpectedly thoughtful, that it completely wrecks me. I press my lips together, trying to hold back the tears threatening to spill over.

"I'm done with it, I swear," I whisper, the words more a plea than a promise.

"You've said that before," Finn replies, his voice tinged with skepticism.

I look at him earnestly, my eyes begging him to believe me.

"I know, but this time I really mean it—I didn't want last night."

"How many times have you said that? Damn it, Cas, you know these guys are just using you, right?" Finn's voice cracks with a quiet sob, and I'm shocked to see tears welling up in his eyes. I've never made him cry before, and the sight of it breaks something inside me.

I get up, go over to him, and pull him into a tight embrace, the weight of my guilt pressing down on me like a vise.

"I'm sorry, I promise it'll be different now. I'm done with it, I swear!" I murmur in his ear, the words coming out in a rush of desperation. Damn it, I don't want this shit anymore.

His arms tighten around me, and I can feel his body trembling under the weight of his concern and my guilt. I never meant to hurt my best friend like this, never wanted to push him to the point of breaking.

Things have changed between us since that summer with Val. Finn was always there for me. Yeah, we ended up in bed together a few times, but it was more than that—less about physical attraction, more about a real friendship that grew out of it. I can tell Finn everything—about the nights I lost myself, even about Val. He knows all my screw-ups, knows how much I missed Val, and yet he didn't judge me. Maybe he knew that if he had, I would've shut down completely like I did with my parents. But now—not even Finn can take it anymore.

I pull back a bit, looking into his familiar brown eyes, now brimming with tears. Gently, I wipe them away with my fingers.

"Get your life together, yeah?" he sighs, and slowly, the sadness in his gaze begins to fade, replaced by a quiet determination.

"I will. No more drugs, no more random guys, no more Cave, I promise," I say, the words feeling like a lifeline, something to hold onto in the midst of the chaos.

He nods, a small, sad smile tugging at the corners of his mouth.

"And talk to Val," he adds softly.

I swallow hard, the mere mention of Val's name sending a fresh wave of pain through me.

"Why?" I whisper, though I already know his answer. I'm not sure I can handle it without feeling that pain again, the wound still too raw.

Finn looks at me with a heavy heart, his eyes filled with a compassion I don't deserve.

"Because it all started with him."

Kapitel 15

Being back here, in the place I once dismissed so easily;
Back here, where the summer breeze still carries a chill, even in August;
Back here, knowing that soon I'll see you again—
It feels unreal, like a dream I've lived over and over in the quiet of night.
Yet fear grips me—
That the weight of what's unspoken will suffocate me,

That you'll look at me the way you did that first time.
Ice cold.

*

No, what followed after my vacation—after my departure—was anything but a happy ending. After that incredible week, when nothing and no one could come between us, we never saw each other again. It felt like a deep cut, the sudden separation, the abrupt distance, the physical withdrawal. Like an icy cold wrapping around me, freezing my thoughts, making it hard to think clearly in the days that followed. It was like falling into a void. Everything inside and around me felt numb, and the pain was unbearable—but at least, back then, there was still hope. Hope that I'd see him again.

In the beginning, Val texted me almost every day. We talked on the phone, sharing our plans and dreams—our future. At first, I was genuinely excited for him. Seeing his success unfold on Instagram felt like watching a dream come true.

Val had plans to move out, away from his father. He was set on selling the Mustang he inherited from his grandfather to cover the deposit for an apartment and a new studio. He wanted to start producing bands again—and see me as often as possible.

Not long after, one of the first bands he produced in his new studio was FiveTunes—the same band we'd seen perform on the beach, the ones who had witnessed my less-than-memorable moment by the sea.

No one, not even Val, could have predicted how quickly their success would take off. It hit him hard, and with it, everything changed—his entire life and, not long after, our relationship, which started unraveling. I was thrilled for him at first, but I could already sense the shift between us, like something was pulling us apart. The growing distance felt like an uncrossable divide, and every time we missed a call, it felt like we were adding another brick to the wall separating us. Val became more distant, and soon, he stopped talking about when we'd see each other again.

In essence, he'd achieved his dream. He got out of his hometown and, thanks to his success and the money he earned, gained independence. He traveled across Europe, spending one night in Paris and the next in London, while I mostly learned about it through his Instagram profile. I remember one post vividly: Val, standing in front of the Eiffel Tower, the city lights making his blue hair glow even brighter. He looked happy, radiant even, but all I could feel was a growing emptiness inside me. Meanwhile, my life remained the same, day in and day out—or at least it seemed that way from the outside.

During the day, I kept going to school, studying for my exams, getting my driver's license, but at night—when I missed him the most—I drove to Cologne, to the Cave, and found the distraction I so desperately needed. The Cave was a different world, a place where I could lose myself in the music, the flashing lights, and the bodies moving around me. It was a place where I didn't have to think about Val, or the life he was living without me.

Dinner at home had become a minefield of silence and forced smiles. My father barely looked at me anymore, his silence louder than any argument we'd ever had. My mother tried to bridge the gap with small talk and smiles that never reached her eyes, but the weight of their disappointment hung in the air, suffocating.

Finn was right—I should have found the courage to go see him much earlier. But every time I brought it up during a phone call, the plans always fell through. Something always came up for Val.

I don't think he did it on purpose; he really did want to see me. In the end, it turned into a whole year where we didn't see each other.

My gaze sweeps over the campsite, filled with tents and caravans. The air is filled with the scent of grilled meat, mixed with the salty tang of the sea. I see the many families sitting outside, having dinner, hear their laughter, their voices, and I can almost feel the carefree holiday atmosphere of the place. The sky is tinged with the warm hues of sunset, and for a moment, I'm transported back to last summer. It's like a déjà vu, seeing myself sitting with my family in front of the camper. The thought of them hurts. I've let them down so often over the past year, broken promises, and lied. Every room in the house felt like a trap, the walls closing in on me with the weight of their expectations. I couldn't take another day of their disappointed looks, the silent judgments that clung to me like a second skin. Moving out wasn't just a plan; it was a lifeline.

I've been saving every penny I can. Once my exams are over, I'm determined to move out—anything to escape their disappointed looks. I want to live my life without having to explain every misstep to them. Naturally, they have no idea I'm back here, up north.

It would have raised too many questions. My parents have long labeled Val as persona non grata, blaming him as the cause of my out-of-control life. Yet, I could never truly forget him. His bright blue eyes still linger in my dreams, and sometimes, I swear I can feel his touch. Val became a ghost in my mind, haunting my thoughts both day and night. No matter how hard I tried, I couldn't escape him, couldn't let him go.

I had to come back here—I need to finally sort out the chaos inside me, to have one last chance at closure, even if my hope is barely hanging on. If things go badly, I'll be back home by tomorrow morning, no harm done. But if it goes well... I can picture it, though the fantasy feels distant, hard to pin down. I'm a dreamer, always have been. I can almost see us on the beach, talking like we used to, with the waves crashing softly in the background. But the image slips away, like trying to hold water in my hands.

Right now, I don't know much about Val's life or what he's been up to. Even his posts have become fewer and fewer over the past few months. I only know from his last post three weeks ago that this week he's recording and mixing a new song for FiveTunes. He'll be here—he has to be.

*

The heavy iron door creaks as it opens, then slams shut far too loudly behind me. The sudden noise echoes in the empty hallway, sending a jolt of panic through me. I flinch, standing in the darkness, my breath quickening as I struggle to find the light switch. My fingers fumble along the cold, rough wall until they finally make contact with the switch. The fluorescent lights above me flicker on with a harsh buzz, revealing a long, narrow corridor that seems to stretch endlessly ahead. The walls are lined with peeling paint, and the air is thick with the smell of dust and something metallic.

The muffled music reaches my ears, a deep bassline thumping rhythmically, accompanied by the faint, raspy voice of a man singing. The sound vibrates through the walls, unsettling me further. Panic grips my chest like a vise, and for a moment, I'm paralyzed, torn between the urge to flee and the desperate need to move forward.

I should turn around and leave—right now. But my feet feel cemented to the floor, my mind racing with what-ifs. What will he say when he sees me after all this time? What will he think? My heart pounds in my chest as a flood of emotions washes over me—fear, regret, longing, all tangled together in a confusing mess. I've replayed this moment in my mind so many times, imagining every possible scenario, but now that it's here, I'm frozen, drowning in a sea of uncertainty.

I swallow hard as the door to the recording studio at the end of the hallway suddenly swings open, and there he is—Val. He stands there, backlit by the dim light spilling from the room behind him, his silhouette sharp and familiar. My breath catches in my throat as our eyes lock, and for a moment, the world around us seems to stand still.

He's exactly as I remember—blue hair, piercing eyes, and that unmistakable presence that draws you in, making it impossible to look away. But there's something different in his gaze, something that wasn't there before—a flicker of emotion I can't quite place. Is it shock? Joy? Or something else entirely?

Whatever it is, it's gone as quickly as it appeared, replaced by a cool, guarded expression.

"Casper," he finally breathes, his voice so quiet, but it still sends a shiver down my spine. The few meters between us feel like an uncrossable chasm, even though he's right there, so close yet so far.

I want to say something, anything, but the words won't come. I just stand there, staring at him, my mind racing, my heart aching. He's still so beautiful, so perfect, and it hurts more than I expected. I can feel the sting of tears behind my eyes, but I blink them back, refusing to let them fall. Not here. Not now.

Val shakes his head slowly, and I feel something inside me crumble, like a fragile structure collapsing under the weight of too much pressure.

"Why are you here?" His voice is flat, emotionless, and it cuts through me like a knife.

Shit. It doesn't even sound like a question. More like an accusation. Like I've done something wrong just by being here.

My chest tightens as the pain surges forward, relentless, spilling over in the form of hot tears that I can't hold back any longer. I thought I was prepared for this, but clearly, I was wrong. He never expected to see me again—I'm nothing more than a distant memory, something he's moved on from.

My mind screams at me to leave, to run, but my legs won't listen. I'm stuck, rooted to the spot, unable to move.

Finally, I manage to turn around, yanking the heavy door open with trembling hands. I step outside, feeling the chill of the evening air against my skin. The industrial landscape around me is bleak, desolate, a far cry from the warmth and vibrancy of the beach where we first met. It mirrors the emptiness I've felt inside for so long.

I force myself to walk, one foot in front of the other, trying to focus on the simple act of moving forward. But every step feels like a battle, my thoughts swirling with the urge to look back, to cling to the hope that he might call out to me, that he might still care.

It's only when I feel a hand on my shoulder that I stop, my heart skipping a beat. I don't dare turn around, not yet. The familiar touch sends a jolt through me, a mix of longing and fear.

"Hey, Cas, wait!" His voice is urgent, almost pleading, and it takes everything in me not to break down right then and there. My breath catches, and for a split second, all the walls I've built up threaten to crumble.

I close my eyes, berating myself for coming back, for putting myself through this all over again.

"Just listen to me for a moment, okay?" His words are soft, almost gentle, but there's a tension in his voice that I can't ignore.

Slowly, I turn to face him, flinching slightly as our gazes meet again. He's so close now, too close, and the intensity of it all takes my breath away. I can feel his warmth, his presence, and it's overwhelming.

"What?" I ask, my voice shaky, barely holding it together. And suddenly, it hits me—this might be the last time we ever see each other.

He looks at me helplessly, his hands hanging at his sides as if he doesn't know what to do with them.

"What did you expect?" His tone is softer now, almost resigned.

I glare at him, anger and pain bubbling up inside me, threatening to spill over.

"We haven't seen each other for over a year! And suddenly you're here, out of nowhere."

"Out of nowhere? You're the one who kept pushing me away all the time!" My voice rises, the frustration I've been bottling up for so long finally breaking free.

He shakes his head, his expression pained. "I thought you understood! Damn it, you even said it yourself."

"Oh yeah?" I snap, the bitterness in my words cutting through the air like a blade. Of course, I tried to support him, I was happy for him, but I never thought that meant the end of us.

"Damn it, Cas." Val crosses his arms over his chest, his posture defensive, closed off.

“What, did you think I’d be thrilled that you completely wrote me off, sacrificed me for your damn career?” My voice is laced with sarcasm, but underneath it is a raw, aching hurt.

“You haven’t changed. Not one bit—you’re still so stubborn, so—” He stops himself, the unspoken words hanging in the air between us.

I should turn around and leave. I should walk away and never look back. But I can’t. Not when he’s standing there, so close, yet so far away. Val has become the ice-cold person I met back then again. Maybe he’s found his passion, his drive, but that’s not me. I never was, and I never will be.

Suddenly, I think of Zoe—the girl who died in the accident with Val. Maybe it was only in her final moments that she truly realized who Val was and what their relationship had really cost her.

I won’t make the same mistake. I won’t sacrifice my life for Val’s.

“I know!” I shout, my voice breaking. “I was naive and stupid to fall for an idiot like you. To spend a whole year hoping you’d finally make an effort and visit me!”

I pause, my chest heaving as I struggle to hold back the tears that are threatening to spill over again. “That I was dumb enough to believe you felt the same way. That was foolish. Fuck, I wasted a whole year—on you!” I shake my head, disbelief and self-loathing mingling in my thoughts.

Val sighs, running a hand through his hair, his face etched with exhaustion.

“We had bad timing. You met me when I was completely down—”

“True, you were a complete mess," I cut him off, "but it didn’t matter because I saw something underneath that thick layer of ice you put up. I felt something... something I stupidly mistook for real feelings.”

The tears finally break free, running down my cheeks, and I hate that I’m showing him how much he hurt me, how much I still care.

Val’s eyes widen slightly, a flicker of guilt crossing his features.

My thoughts drift back to my birthday last week. I spent the whole day hoping Val would at least send a short “Happy Birthday.” But nothing came—absolutely nothing. I don’t matter to him anymore. I’m just a distant memory, a chapter he’s closed and moved on from.

"Now I'm the one who's completely broken, and of course, you can't deal with baggage like me anymore!" I spit out, my words laced with bitterness.

Val takes a deep breath, his shoulders sagging as if the weight of his own words is too much to carry. "God, believe me, I wish it were easier—I wish *I* were easier." His voice is soft, almost pleading. "You're not someone anyone could ever forget, Cas, never." His eyes flicker with something—regret, maybe—but just as quickly, he looks away, unable to hold my gaze.

"But I had no damn clue how to balance this—us—with my work. Shit, even now, I have to leave for London tomorrow."

"You didn't even try!" I growl, the anger bubbling up inside me again.

"Cas, damn it, our lives are so different—you're still in school, you want to go to university—I don't want to hold you back from anything, not from meeting someone else or changing your life—for me!"

His words hit me like a punch to the gut, leaving me breathless. There's a part of me that wants to believe him, that wants to hope, but another part of me knows that hope is dangerous. It's a double-edged sword that cuts deeper the longer you hold onto it.

"So what are we, really? Or maybe, what *was* this for you?" I ask, my voice trembling under the weight of it.

Val doesn't answer right away, his eyes searching mine for something—understanding, forgiveness, maybe.

"I honestly don't know… Casper, damn it, I think about you, about our incredible time here, so often… but I don't have an answer. I can't ask you to wait for me or promise that this, us, could ever be more—I—" He breaks off, his voice trailing into silence.

"I know," I murmur, the shame and regret washing over me like a wave.

We never even talked about being in a 'relationship' after I left. It felt too distant, too out of reach, and I don't believe long-distance can really work anyway. What Val and I had was built on touches, those amazing kisses, and that mind-blowing sex.

We had a really strong connection that week last summer—something intense—but there was no way to keep that going with us being hundreds of miles apart.

I wasn't tied to Val, and he wasn't tied to me.

And I spent a long time searching for someone like Val, but everyone I found and shared a bed with didn't spark even a fraction of what I felt with him back then.

I close my eyes, trying to shut everything out. But then I suddenly feel Val's warm fingers on my waist, then on my neck. He pulls me closer, and I can feel his heart pounding hard and fast against my chest.

"But I can't just let you walk away now, either." His lips brush lightly against my skin, sending a shiver down my spine.

"Fuck, I can't give you anything, can't promise you anything, not a damn thing," he breathes into my ear.

All I can do is hum softly. Feeling him now, so clearly again—I can't resist. My fingers tangle in his hair, feeling his lips on my neck, his breath on my skin. I missed it so much.

It won't work, this thing between us, and yet here we are. Unable to let go of each other.

Val's lips trail along my jaw, moving higher until they finally meet mine. I kiss him hungrily, a soft whimper escaping me, filled with need. Nothing has faded—not the intensity, not the spark. Val still tastes just like he did a year ago—like a stormy, heated summer, pure desire, and absolute happiness.

His tongue slides into me, taking me over, and we battle, pressing our bodies against each other, clutching each other like we're two magnets drawn together. I taste him, smell him—so clearly, Val's unmistakable scent, that sharp note that shakes me to my core.

A needy moan escapes me when he briefly pulls away. Immediately, I pull him back close, digging my fingers into his hips.

"Doesn't matter," I whisper. "You don't have to promise me anything!"

Val puts some distance between us again, shaking his head, but his hand stays on my neck.

"You're worth more than that, okay? Don't waste your life on me."

I glare at him stubbornly like a child. But I can't help it—not with him.

"I'm not wasting anything!" I groan. "Just let me come with you, to London!" It's a wild, spur-of-the-moment idea—absolutely insane. No way will Val say yes.

He looks at me with doubt in his eyes. Desperate to avoid the answer, I press my body against his, wrapping my arms around him, finding his lips again. I don't want to hear the words, I just want to feel his response.

*

In the dead of night, we stumble up the narrow stairs next to his studio, our movements wild and reckless. The room above is small, barely furnished with just a bed and a table, but it's all we need. The air is thick with the anticipation of what's to come, every breath charged with the electricity between us.

Val's lips find my neck, sucking hungrily, as his fingers impatiently slide under my t-shirt, nearly tearing it off in his haste. My body trembles, eager and responsive, as I meet him halfway, letting him strip me until I'm lying bare beneath him. His wild eyes rake over every inch of me, his gaze a mix of hunger and possessiveness. When his eyes finally settle on my hard cock, I feel a surge of heat rush through me.

This is his game, and I'm all in, willing to play along. Val, still fully clothed, hovers over me, his presence the only barrier between us. I can sense his need for control, his desire to dominate, and I willingly surrender to it, giving him the power he seeks. In this moment, nothing else matters—only his touch, the way he makes me feel alive again.

"Do whatever you want with me," I whisper, my voice thick with desire. The words barely escape my lips before Val responds with a hoarse, uncontrolled moan. His hands grip mine, pinning them to the bed, and then he kisses me—hard and demanding. I squirm beneath him, desperate for more than just his lips, craving the full weight of his body against mine. But Val keeps control, his strength a reminder that tonight, he's in charge.

"Stay like that," he hisses, pulling away from me completely. He stands at the edge of the bed, his eyes locked on mine, and my heart races with a mix of excitement and anticipation. It feels like our first time all over again, like I'm that inexperienced boy trembling with the thrill of the unknown. I obey, keeping my hands above my head as if they're tied there, my body aching for his touch.

"Come back and touch me," I whisper, my voice barely audible.

Val takes a deep breath, his chest rising and falling as he struggles to maintain his composure. "Why do you smell so damn good?" he murmurs, his words laced with a kind of desperation.

A playful snort escapes me. "What do I smell like?" I grin, lifting my head slightly to meet his gaze.

Val leans back onto the bed, propping himself up beside my head, his eyes so intense that they steal the breath from my lungs.

"Indescribable. Like cotton candy, raspberries, and asphalt, with something else I can't even name. Fuck." He leans in, inhaling deeply, his mouth and nose trailing over my skin, leaving a path of goosebumps in their wake.

Unconsciously, I start to tremble, shivering not from cold but from the overwhelming joy of being touched by him again. Val clings to me, tasting me, his lips and tongue moving lower over my collarbone, down my chest, not stopping until my throbbing erection is nestled between his lips. A groan of approval escapes him, the sound vibrating through me.

His tongue flicks over my tip, savoring the precum that leaks out. I'm helpless, my body frozen in place, my eyes wide with amazement as I watch him worship me with every flick of his tongue, every gentle suck. I whimper, the sound almost pitiful as the emotions I've kept locked away for so long bubble to the surface. I missed him so much, missed this connection that I can't find with anyone else.

The things I did to forget him, the ways I tried to fill the void he left, seem so foolish now. But that's all in the past—right now, it's just us, and it feels perfect. No one else will ever come close to making me feel the way Val does.

A choked sound escapes me as Val takes my cock deep into his mouth, a long, drawn-out "fuck" slipping from my lips as he repeats the motion. He lets my cock slide almost completely out before taking me deep again, the sensation making my toes curl in the sheets. All I can do is lean back and let him take over, giving in to the pleasure he's so easily making me feel.

Val takes me to places I never thought possible, turning everything in my head into a sticky, sweet haze. His devotion, his passion, the constant moan slipping from his lips as he sucks on me—it's not just physical. The look on his face, the pure pleasure etched in his features, shows nothing but genuine enjoyment, absolute desire. I'm teetering on the edge, the pressure inside me building to a point where I know I can't hold back much longer.

"Fuck, Val, I'm coming!" I gasp, my hands tangling in his soft hair as I push him down, letting him taste everything that spills out of me. He doesn't resist, just swallows and swallows, taking in more than he can handle. It drips from the corners of his mouth, down his chin, and onto both of us, but he doesn't stop—he keeps going as if this were only the beginning. His fingers swipe through my cum, spreading it between my cheeks, and I hiss, panting, pushing back against him. Val presses his thumb against my entrance, prolonging the waves of my orgasm, making them seem endless. I arch my back, completely lost in the sensation, feeling nothing but pure, unadulterated pleasure.

*

His fingers slip inside me, stretching me, getting me ready. But everything already feels so soft, warm, and sweet, like my body was made for this, for him. A needy whimper escapes me, a plea for more. I want him deep inside me, filling me completely.

"Val," I moan, my voice thick with need. That's all I need to say. Val kneels over me, yanking his t-shirt off, followed clumsily by his pants and boxers. Then he's back on top of me, spreading my legs apart and sliding his body over mine. Our cocks brush against each other, and a loud moan escapes Val as his forehead presses against mine.

"I want you so bad," he whispers, the words a confession, a promise, and all the apology I need. I'm as deeply under Val's skin as he is under mine. I don't care about tomorrow—only this moment matters, and I'll hold onto it for as long as I can.

His hand slides lower, wrapping around his cock, rubbing it between my thighs, sliding lower until the tip brushes against my entrance. I let out an approving gasp, bending my legs to give him the angle he needs to finally push inside me.

He pauses, looking down at me.

"It's okay, really," I whisper, my hand reaching up to touch his face.

"I..." Guilt flashes in his eyes, but I place my fingers over his lips, silencing him. A second later, every muscle in Val's body tightens as he pushes inside me, deeper and deeper, until he's fully buried in me, filling me completely.

The small room fills with our gasps and moans, the sound of skin against skin. We're nothing but a mass of lust and desire, and every thrust Val gives is met with a desperate moan that presses me deeper into the mattress. My fingers instinctively find his ass, gripping it, feeling the tension with every thrust he makes inside me. His head is buried between my neck and shoulder.

"Cas," he murmurs, his voice strained. "Fuck, Cas!" It's not just lust in his voice—there's also pain. Emotional pain. His arms wrap around my neck and back, holding me as close as possible, as if he's afraid I might disappear, that all of this is just a dream.

I smile blissfully to myself, feeling a deep sense of happiness, of contentment. His lips travel over my neck, up to my chin. He looks into my eyes, and there's so much fire in his gaze now.

"Like last time," he murmurs, and I know immediately what he wants. What I want. The same control over him that he has over me right now. My fingers move lower, between his cheeks, rubbing over his most sensitive spot as Val relentlessly pumps into me, wild and uninhibited.

"I'm close," he hisses, pressing his lips against my neck, sucking on it. As if that's my cue, I push him off me and roll out from under him, only to be on top of him the next moment, spreading his legs and pressing my lips between his cheeks.

A long, drawn-out "fuck" escapes him as I run my tongue over his sensitive ring. He surrenders completely, spreading his legs wide and lifting his hips, giving me everything he has.

My fingers slide inside him, alternating with my tongue, and Val is swept away by a wave of pleasure. He suddenly comes, gasping hard, moaning, and trembling. Immediately, I'm on his cock, wrapping my mouth around his tip, swallowing his cum as three fingers disappear between his legs, turning Val into a helpless, whimpering mess. I feel the pure lust coursing through him, drawing it out—continuing with my fingers and tongue until Val finally collapses on the bed in front of me, breathless and almost paralyzed.

The room spins slightly as I stare up at the low ceiling, feeling the warmth of Val's body pressed against mine. It's a sensation that makes me feel lightheaded, like I'm back on that old boat where Val took me once—everything sways, and I'm caught in the gentle rocking, lost in the moment. But here, in his arms, I feel something indescribable, a comfort that words can't capture. No explanations are needed between us, just the language of our bodies, our overwhelming desire for each other that speaks louder than anything we could say.

Val's breath is warm against my neck, and I feel him inhale deeply, as if he's trying to memorize my scent. "Raspberries and asphalt," he murmurs, and I grin to myself, feeling foolishly content, as though this small, odd detail is something sacred between us.

"I bet there are a few people in your hometown who've gone crazy for you just like I did," he says suddenly, his voice low and thoughtful.

I snort, the sound echoing in the quiet room, and turn my head to look at him, arching an eyebrow. "What's that supposed to mean?"

"That there are others," he replies matter-of-factly, and for a brief moment, Finn's face flashes in my mind. Finn, the voice of reason, my best friend who would probably cheer at the sight of me finally finding my way back to Val and lying here with him.

The summer with Val, my first time—everything changed after that. It awakened something inside me, a curiosity I didn't know I had. About my body, about sex, about connections that run deeper than I ever thought possible.

But Val was far away, always out of reach. Finn became my lifeline, the boy I turned to a few weeks after Val and I had last been together. I slept with him to feel a closeness to Val, even if it was just for a fleeting second, even if it was just in the moment of release when I closed my eyes and saw Val's face instead.

"Does it matter?" I ask, trying to sound indifferent, though the words catch in my throat.

He shrugs, his expression thoughtful, as if he's weighing something in his mind. "Is there someone?" he finally asks, his fingers lightly tracing the line between my collarbone and shoulder, sending shivers down my spine.

"You sound jealous," I tease, watching the way his eyes close briefly, his long lashes fluttering against his cheeks. An unconscious laugh escapes me, and I sit up, turning to face him fully. He really does seem agitated, and for a moment, I enjoy seeing him like this—vulnerable, uncertain.

"You're the one who told me not to wait for you," I remind him, the words tinged with a hint of bitterness.

He snorts, frustration evident in the sound. "There's a big difference between saying something and actually doing it!"

"God," I scoff, shaking my head in disbelief. "You're really jealous." The realization is almost amusing, but the seriousness in his eyes keeps me grounded. Val crosses his arms over his chest, a defensive gesture that only confirms my suspicions.

"Honestly, you can't tell me there was no one this year," he urges, his tone a mix of curiosity and something darker.

I snort, deflecting his question. "And you?" I ask. Val shakes his head almost imperceptibly. "I've already told you how I feel about dating and one-night stands. They don't mean anything to me," he says, his voice steady, though I can sense the underlying tension.

"Yeah, but you also said you had some before we met," I reply, my voice softer, almost hesitant. Val's gaze hardens as he wrestles with his thoughts, deciding how much he wants to share. Finally, he closes his eyes as if to compose himself, then sighs deeply.

"Yeah, okay? Yes, there was someone I dated for a short time," he admits, his voice sounding frustrated, almost apologetic. "But it didn't even last a month!"

Surprisingly, the jealousy I expected never comes. Instead, I feel curious. "A guy or a girl?" I ask, my tone playful, almost teasing. "A girl," he sighs, and I can't help but grin.

"I honestly thought you'd be more curious," I quip, but Val's expression doesn't change. "Cas, damn it!" he says softly, his frustration evident. "Seems like you were the more curious one."

I roll my eyes, exhaling sharply. "You're so hard to figure out. You avoid me for over a year and then get jealous because I had sex with others."

Val presses his hands against his face, groaning in exasperation.

"I know," he mutters, his voice muffled by his hands, and for a moment, the room falls into silence again, thick with unspoken words.

"And how many were there?" he asks quietly, his voice breaking the silence, the weight of the question hanging between us.

I stare at him, the memories flashing through my mind—nights spent chasing after something I couldn't quite grasp, trying to fill the void Val left behind. Curiosity and distraction—that's what it was. A mix that drove my parents and Finn insane.

Nights where I vanished, only to return in the morning, blinded by the daylight, filled with shame, regret, and disbelief. On those nights, I wasn't Casper, not Cas—I was someone else entirely, someone I couldn't bear to look at in the light of day.

Finn was the beginning. Later, I went alone to the gay clubs in Cologne, places like the Cave. It was intense, no boundaries, no taboos. That's the best way to describe it.

I let loose, and while it was thrilling at first, it was always just a brief escape from my messed-up life and from Val. It's not something I need anymore, not when I'm here with him. Nothing I wouldn't give up in a heartbeat if it meant we could have something real again. I did it out of desperation, and I almost always regretted it afterward. Just thinking about it now tears me apart.

"God," I sigh, looking at him, nervously chewing on my lip. I should keep all of this to myself, but that's never been how things are between us—no lies, no secrets. Val told me everything, even about the worst moment of his life, his greatest loss, his great love, Zoe. He'll understand what I did—he has to.

"I occasionally slept with my best friend, Finn," I begin, my voice hesitant, unsure how he'll react.

He tilts his head slightly, doubt flickering in his eyes.

"And sometimes I went out to a few clubs in Cologne at night, met guys there, and, well, you can probably guess the rest..." I have to swallow hard, forcing the words out, saying it out loud and honestly for the first time.

Val takes a deep breath, and I can see the struggle in him, the way he fights to stay calm. His jaw tightens, his eyes searching mine, and I look at him sincerely, hoping he can see the truth in my gaze.

"But it doesn't matter, not here, not now, not anymore, okay?" I say, my voice trembling slightly as I reach for his hand, panicking at the thought that he might get up and leave, that he might send me away. I can't lose him, not now, not after everything.

"I was curious, and I missed you so damn much. I needed that distraction on those nights," I confess, my hand moving to his cheek, feeling the warmth of his skin under my palm. Val grips my hand, holding it tightly, and I look at him with hope, praying he'll understand.

"It was never like it is with you. I never felt what I feel with you," I whisper, the words heavy with emotion. They sit on the tip of my tongue, but I can't bring myself to say them out loud. Instead, I interlace my fingers with his, letting the silence speak for us. My heart pounds so loudly in my chest that I'm sure he can hear it, too.

"God, Cas," he murmurs finally, his voice soft, a faint smile tugging at his lips. "I wish I could have both—you and—" He gestures around the room, the studio, the life he's built for himself. "This."

I exhale in relief, the tension easing slightly from my shoulders.

"Then let me be a part of it. We don't have to see each other all the time; I can come to you. It's fine, really," I say, desperate to make this work, to hold on to whatever we have.

He presses his lips together, and I can see the conflict in his eyes. "Casper," he sighs, and I brace myself for the worst. "I want to be honest with you—the thought of you with someone else while we're apart..." He runs a hand over his forehead, letting go of mine. "Maybe I'm old-fashioned, or something, but it tears me apart. The idea of sharing you, the way those guys look at you... Fuck, I just couldn't deal with it," he groans, his frustration clear.

I shake my head, sadness giving way to a rising anger. "You sound like you're from another time!" I scoff, the words slipping out before I can stop them. "Honestly, what choice did you leave me? Maybe you can go without sex, without touch, without intimacy, but I can't!" The cold fury grips me, making my voice sharp.

Val still feels like a dead end; I'm not going to promise to give all that up only to wait endlessly for him to make a move. Why is he so contradictory? Telling me not to hold back, not to wait, then reacting like a jealous idiot when I'm honest about being with others. I'll never understand him.

Sure, I know I went too far on many nights—I can cut back, but no sex at all? When he's gone for months? No. He can't ask that of me.

I stand up silently, collecting my clothes while Val watches in silence.

It's only when I'm dressed again that he speaks, his voice softer, almost apologetic. "I'll work on it, okay?"

I pause, questioning, searching his face for sincerity.

"I won't let another year go by without seeing you again. I'll come to visit you in the next few weeks. And I'm glad you were honest with me." He closes his eyes briefly, as if gathering himself. "I'll learn to deal with it."

I tilt my head, still uncertain, studying him.

Val shrugs, a hint of resignation in his posture. "Then we'll have an open relationship. It's better than nothing. Shit." He stands, stepping closer, and gently grabs my chin, lifting it so our eyes meet.

"I'm crazy about you—you should know that by now. And I'm so glad you're here, braver than I am..." He swallows hard. "Because I could never have sent you away," he murmurs.

Doubtfully, I bite my lip. "Really?"

"Really," he says, his nod firm, eyes sincere.

A relieved smile crosses my face. My fingers trace his forehead, his cheek, every inch until they finally reach his lips. Val catches my thumb, sucking on it with a look that says he wants to devour me whole. A shiver runs through me, so intense, so uncontrollable. Val's eyelids flutter, and the blue in his eyes deepens, darkens with desire.

"Fuck me," he whispers, his voice thick with need. "And come with me to London tomorrow."

I grin and pull him into a hug as we tumble back onto the bed, laughter filling the space between us. In no time, my clothes are off, and I'm lying on top of this wild, blue-haired boy who ignites every fiber of my being.

I kiss him hungrily, and he instinctively melts into me beneath the sheets. My fingers slide back between his cheeks, already preparing him, but he feels so smooth and ready at his entrance.

I have the control, over Val's body, over every move he makes—now and maybe even in the future.

I take the opportunity to hook his left leg up, slipping my hands under his ass, lifting him slightly, and positioning my hard cock right at his entrance.

"Do it," he hisses, encouraging me as if he hadn't just had a mind-blowing orgasm. How could I resist? How could I even think of stopping now?

I push inside, and the tight heat wraps around me. I have to bite down hard on my bottom lip to keep from coming instantly. It's so good, so unbelievably good.

Everything inside me pulls tight; God, I missed him. I missed his body, his mind, everything that makes him who he is. My stomach buzzes and hums. I'm hopelessly, undeniably in love with him.

I push deeper while Val watches me with that wild, burning look in his eyes—desire that refuses to fade.

"Fuck, I missed you so much," he whispers as I fill him completely, leaning over him, staring at him like I'm hypnotized.

His fingers trace my cheek. "I was such an idiot!"

I swallow hard, nodding just slightly before I start to move. Thrusting into him the way he did earlier—hard, without hesitation or pause. Val takes every thrust, responding to each with a deep, dark moan.

I don't know if what we have can even be compared to anything else. For me, it's so much more than just sex. Val and I—there are no boundaries when we're together, when we lose ourselves in each other. He's mine, and I'm his, absolutely. There's no shame, no hesitation like there was in the beginning. We're completely equal. Maybe that's what makes being with him feel so unique.

The words tingle in my throat, pushing up toward my lips. They want to spill out, just like the explosion building between my legs.

I capture his lips, trying to silence the words, but Val gently pushes me back, staring up at me. Suddenly, everything goes quiet—no moaning, no panting—just the heavy breathing between us.

"What?" I ask hesitantly.

He smiles softly, but there's that flash of pain in his eyes again. "You know what."

My eyes flicker. I know he's talking about my feelings for him. But he's already had his great love—after such a traumatic loss, is it even possible for him to feel something like that again? For me?

His fingers stroke my cheek as if confirming my thoughts.

He blinks and nods slightly. He doesn't need to say it out loud. In that moment, I know it without any more words. What we have is something so special, so rare—that he loves me, and I love him.

Val presses closer against me, his body sliding against mine with a desperation that's almost palpable. His breath is ragged, his eyes locked onto mine as if I'm the only thing tethering him to reality. The intensity in his gaze makes my heart race, as if the unspoken words between us are more powerful than anything we've ever said out loud. The world outside fades away until it's just us—our bodies, our breathing, the undeniable pull that has always been there.

He moves beneath me, his hips meeting mine in perfect rhythm. Every inch of him fits so perfectly around me, as if we're made to fit this way. His skin is slick with sweat, warm beneath my fingertips as I grip his hips tighter, pulling him closer, as close as physically possible. His body responds to mine with such fluidity that it's like he knows exactly what I need before I even do.

Val's voice is low and hoarse as he whispers my name, the sound trembling with a mixture of urgency and affection. It's the kind of voice that could undo every ounce of control I have left, and it does. My vision blurs, the room spinning as all I can focus on is him—his soft lips parted in pleasure, his hands clinging to my shoulders like he's afraid I'll vanish.

I can feel his muscles tightening around me, every movement drawing me deeper, and it's almost too much to handle. He's shaking, gasping, caught somewhere between surrender and ecstasy. My own release builds like a tidal wave, unstoppable, crashing over me with a force that leaves me breathless. I bury myself in him, groaning into the curve of his neck as I come hard, the pleasure searing through every nerve in my body.

But it doesn't stop there. The way he moans my name again, the way his nails dig into my back, keeps me on edge. I hold him closer, needing to feel every tremor as he teeters on the edge. I can sense it—the way his breathing hitches, his body tensing beneath mine—and then he's there, letting go. Val's back arches, his mouth falling open in a silent cry as he comes, his release hot and sticky between us. The rawness of it, the way he completely surrenders in that moment, takes my breath away.

He collapses against the sheets, his chest heaving as he rides out the aftershocks. His legs are still wrapped around my waist, refusing to let go, as if we're still scared of the distance that once separated us. I don't pull away either, not yet. I can feel him pulsing around me, the last echoes of his climax drawing me in, keeping me grounded in this moment with him.

For a few seconds, we're lost in each other—just breathing, just feeling. His fingers trace lazily over my shoulders, and I can't help but press one last kiss to his lips, savoring the way he melts into it, the way he tastes like home and belonging. It's not just about the sex. It's the way everything in the world feels right when we're like this—connected, complete.

When I finally pull back, our eyes meet again, and the look in his gaze is softer now—less guarded, more vulnerable. There's still so much left unsaid between us, but for now, in this fleeting moment, nothing else matters.

Epilogue

In the past few months, I've memorized Val's schedule completely. I know when he's in the studio, when he's working as a DJ, and when he has his days off. Knowing all of this gives me a sense of security I never had during that year of silence. I trust him, and he trusts me, even when we sometimes don't see each other for weeks.

Not that I've built my entire life around his schedule, but a big part of my mind—aside from my studies and my part-time job—is filled with thoughts of Val. I need him, now more than ever. Especially on the nights when I feel like I'm about to break from longing, when it's so hard not to give in to the urge to go out and lose myself again. But I'm not alone with my problems anymore; I have Finn and Justin, and yes, I can call Val whenever I need to, even in the middle of the night. Even if he doesn't hear it immediately, he always calls back.

It was hard coming back to my life after our incredible weekend in London. There was this huge dark hole threatening to swallow me again, but this time I fought against it and was completely honest—with my friends and even my parents. I didn't want to keep going down that path—no more drugs, no more sex with random jerks just to forget. I wanted Valentin and no one else.

My parents helped me find a good therapist. I went to rehab, stayed in a clinic for three weeks, and even after that, I started attending a support group. Boys and girls my age who met weekly in my hometown and had similar struggles to mine. Listening and talking about it—it helped. I slowly began to heal, and the addiction faded into the background, though I still feel that urge every day, the urge to take the easy way out, to pop a pill or head out to the Cave. My therapist was honest with me and speaks openly about it. She says that it might always be there, that quiet voice inside me whispering to do it again. I can't silence it, but I can drown it out.

I have a carefully structured daily routine. It starts at 6 AM with getting up and a half-hour jog. After breakfast, I head to the sports university, and three evenings a week, I work a shift at the arena in the neighboring city. I like the atmosphere there, even though I usually avoid clubs. I enjoy the lively energy around me—from the sidelines, so to speak. When I'm working at the bar inside, I often stare at the stage and imagine Val up there.

Not that it's his dream to DJ in a massive venue like this—not yet, at least—but I know that if he keeps going like this, he'll be a huge star someday, filling arenas like this one with nearly 30,000 seats.

Val's future is both exciting and terrifying to me. A year has passed since our reunion.

This year I picked myself up again, finished high school and started studying sports science. Getting into the program wasn't easy; the failure rate at sports college is extremely high, but I worked towards it for months and made it on the first try. Thanks to Finn, who trained with me five days a week. Sport, along with Val and my friends, has become my anchor. I am aware of my mistakes, the dark places in my soul, and I want to put them to bed once and for all.

Sure, a year ago, I thought that living recklessly was what I wanted and needed. That I didn't care if I let men use and screw me, that it didn't bother me to wake up in the morning as just a shadow of myself. Hell, if I'd kept going like that, I wouldn't be here today—it would have destroyed me. Finn knew it, just like my parents did. I was the last one to finally understand it. I know how lucky I am that my family never gave up on me, that even after that hellish year, they stood by me and forgave me.

I didn't move out; I'm still living in my room in the attic. And that's okay; it gives me stability, a framework to operate within without spiraling out of control again. But today is an exception. Today is finally Friday, the day I've been looking forward to for weeks. I'm on my way to the airport. I'm finally going to see Val again after more than a month without him. I'm on my way to Berlin for his first big gig in the capital.

*

I weave my way through the pulsating crowd, the air thick with a mix of sweat, cologne, and the electric buzz of anticipation. Bodies sway and press together, lost in the pounding rhythm that vibrates through the floor. The bass thrums so deeply I feel it in my chest, resonating with the wild thrum of my heart as I move closer to the source. Neon lights flash in time with the beat, painting the sea of people in shades of blue, pink, and violet. It's chaos, pure and exhilarating, but there's only one thing anchoring my focus tonight—him.

Pushing past groups of people laughing and shouting over the music, I squeeze my way to the front, where the lights intensify, cutting through the darkness like blades. My gaze locks onto the elevated DJ booth, and there he is—Val. Towering above the mass of bodies like a king commanding his kingdom, his presence alone ignites a spark of excitement that ripples through the room. Even from a distance, I can see the intense concentration etched on his face as he works the controls. He is in his element, completely absorbed in the knobs and sliders beneath his hands, his fingers moving with a precision that speaks of endless hours of practice and passion. The crowd moves in unison with the beats he creates, a sea of raised arms, bobbing heads and ecstatic smiles.

His signature blue hair catches the strobe lights, glowing like a beacon in the night. His left headphone is half-cocked over his ear, and I can see the way his lips curve into that cocky, infectious grin as he drops a heavy bassline that sends a collective shiver through the room. The entire place is alive with his energy, and in that moment, I'm reminded of just how magnetic he is—how the world seems to bend around him when he's in his zone.

Then, like it was preordained, his eyes sweep over the crowd and lock onto mine. It's instant, like gravity pulling us together across the chaotic sea of bodies. My breath catches in my throat as he holds my gaze, and for a split second, the entire room fades away. It's just us—just him and me in this buzzing, vibrating space. I tilt my head, smiling like an idiot because it's impossible not to when I see that familiar spark in his eyes. His grin widens, playful and knowing, as if to say, *I knew you'd be here.* He rolls his eyes in mock exasperation but can't hide the warmth behind it.

Without missing a beat, Val lifts his hand and beckons me with a casual wave, his fingers curling in that subtle, come-here gesture that's impossible to refuse. The invitation is unspoken but clear: *Get up here where you belong.* My pulse races as I squeeze past the last few bodies between us and climb up the narrow steps to join him. The world feels surreal as I close the distance, the music pounding in sync with my heart.

When I reach him, it's like stepping into a different universe. The chaos of the crowd is beneath us now, and all I can see, feel, and smell is Val. He's already reaching for me with one hand still on the controls, as if he can't wait another second. The other hand finds its place around my waist, fingers pressing into the fabric of my t-shirt like he's anchoring himself to me. The touch is firm, reassuring, and sends warmth spreading through my chest. He pulls me closer, his face inches from mine, and in that brief pause, the noise around us melts into the background.

Our eyes meet again, and everything I've felt over the past few weeks—the distance, the longing, the nights spent staring at my phone—fades away. None of it matters when he's this close when I can feel the heat of his breath against my lips. Every doubt, every sleepless night melts away. The warmth of his breath against my lips is all the reassurance I need. There's no need for words, no need for explanations. In the space between us, everything is understood. The familiarity of this moment, the connection we've fought to hold onto despite the time apart, makes me feel like I'm home.

Then he leans in, and our lips meet in a kiss that's slow but intense, a silent promise that says more than any words could. His lips are soft, warm, and the way he lingers on mine, just a little longer than needed, tells me he's missed this as much as I have. It's a kiss filled with everything—the relief of being together again, the joy of closing the distance, and the unspoken certainty that no matter what, we'll find a way through.

The crowd cheers as the beat drops, oblivious to the private moment happening just above their heads, but we're lost in our own world. Val pulls back, his grin widening as he brushes his thumb over my lower lip, his eyes sparkling with mischief and affection. Without saying a word, he turns back to the mixing console, but not before giving my waist a squeeze, a silent reassurance that even in the midst of all this, I'm right where I should be—by his side.

No questions, no words, no fear—I love him.

The End

JULIEN ROUX ONLINE

Find out more about my book releases and upcoming projects on Instagram or Patreon

Julien Roux on Instagram
instagram.com/noenwritesitdown/
Author of queer romance | Writer & Creator
Follow for updates on new books, comics, and more!

Julien Roux on Patreon
Support me on Patreon and be the first to hear about new projects, chapters, illustrations, and updates on the progress of the comic "Fiore – Shadow Creatures."

Printed in Great Britain
by Amazon